Immortal Tyranny

The Judas Chronicles: Book Five

By

Aiden James

Acclaim for Aiden James:

"Aiden James has written a deeply psychological, gripping tale that keeps the readers hooked from page one." *Bookfinds review for "The Forgotten Eden"*

"A variety of twists, surprises, and subplots keep the story moving forward at a good pace. My interest was piqued almost immediately and my attention never wavered as I forced my eyes to stay open well into the night. (Sleep is overrated.) Aiden James is a Master Storyteller, whose career is on the rise! Out-freaking-standing-excellent!" *Detra Fitch of Huntress Reviews, for "Immortal Plague"*

"Aiden James' writing style flows very easily and I found that Cades Cove snowballed into a very gripping tale. Clearly the strengths in the piece were as the spirit's interaction became prevalent with the family.... The Indian lore and ceremonies and the flashbacks to Allie Mae's (earthly) demise were very powerful. I think those aspects separated the work from what we've seen before in horror and ghost tales." *Evelyn Klebert, Author of "A Ghost of a Chance", "Dragonflies", and "An Uneasy Traveler" for "Cades Cove"*

"The intense writing style of Aiden James kept my eyes glued to the story and the pages seemed to fly by at warp speed.... Twists, turns, and surprises pop up at random times to keep the reader off balance. It all blends together to create one of the best stories I have read all year." *Detra Fitch, Huntress Reviews, for "The Devil's Paradise"*

"Aiden James is insanely talented! We are watching a master at work....Ghost stories don't get any better than this." *J.R. Rain,*

Author of "Moon Dance' and "Vampire Moon" for "The Raven Mocker"

BOOKS BY AIDEN JAMES

CADES COVE SERIES
Cades Cove
The Raven Mocker

THE TALISMAN CHRONICLES
The Forgotten Eden
The Devil's Paradise
Hurakan's Chalice (with Mike Robinson)

THE DYING OF THE DARK SERIES
With Patrick Burdine
The Vampires' Last Lover
The Vampires' Birthright
(Coming 2015)
Blood Princesses of the Vampires
(Coming 2016)
Scarlet Legacy of the Vampires
(Coming in 2017)

THE JUDAS CHRONICLES
Immortal Plague
Immortal Reign
Immortal Destiny
Immortal Dragon
Immortal Tyranny
Immortal Pyramid
Immortal Victory

NICK CAINE ADVENTURES
With J.R. Rain
Temple of the Jaguar
Treasure of the Deep
Pyramid of the Gods
Aiden James only
Curse of the Druids
Secret of the Loch
River of the Damned

WITCHES OF DENMARK
The Witches of Denmark
Witch out of Water
(Coming 2015)

WITH MICHELLE WRIGHT
The Judas Reflections
Murder in Whitechapel
Curse of Stigmata
Maid of Heaven
(Coming 2015)

WITH LISA COLLICUTT
The Serendipitous Curse
Reborn
Reviled
Redeemed

WITH JAMES WYMORE
The Actuator: Fractured Earth
The Actuator 2: Return of the Saboteur
(Coming in 2015)

Published 2015
Manor House Books
Paris, Tennessee

Copyright © 2014 by Aiden James
Cover design by Michelle Johnson

All rights reserved

Printed in the United States of America.

First Edition

Immortal Tyranny

~

Aiden James

To all those who live in the hope of eternal redemption.

Immortal Tyranny

Prologue

Greetings from Sedona, Arizona.

I say this *not* without trepidation. After being evicted from our previous lives in Virginia by Krontos Lazarevic, we've spent the past five months looking over our shoulders while searching for a new home. Preferably, it means a haven beyond the voyeuristic reach of our latest, and most deadly, nemesis.

Not an easy proposition, since this enemy holds an enormous advantage over my family—Beatrice, Alistair, and Amy Golden Eagle—and my closest friends, Roderick Cooley and Cedric Tomlinson. As many will recall, Krontos Lazarevic successfully flushed us out of Roderick's splendid underground fortress in Abingdon. He made certain I personally understood his intent to confiscate the twenty-five coins held in my possession. Silver shekels once paid to me for the betrayal of Jesus Christ nearly two thousand years ago. The majority of these coins I have tirelessly hunted down during the past century, and am in no hurry to relinquish. Not a single blood coin, as I like to refer to them, will I hand over without strong incentive to do so!

However, to save my beloved son, Alistair, and the woman I cherish above all others, Beatrice—I would forego my hoped-for redemption and give all twenty-five coins to whoever forcefully demanded them. I would do this, if it could guarantee my family's permanent safety and prosperity. Same thing goes for Amy, Roderick, and Cedric.

But I'm getting ahead of myself.

What follows is not an account that's been resolved. We remain in grave danger. But rather than wait until after reaching a final outcome or after securing the permanent haven we diligently seek, I've decided to bring everyone up to date now on the latest events, and continue on from there.

So, lend me your attention and hold on tight to those you love.

It's what I intend to do.

William

Chapter One

It took almost three months to find a place safe enough to serve as our home. Not a permanent pad, but someplace nice. Cedric had hoped his cousin would put us up in the Indiana farm he mentioned back in Abingdon. But after receiving a less than gracious welcome, we stayed the night and moved on to the rural outskirts of Kansas City. Another farm, this one belonged to a government friend of Roderick's.

I thought we might stay a month or two in this locale. However, when a pair of decomposing red roses was left outside the front door three mornings after our arrival, we were back on the road within the hour. It might've been a strange coincidence for what appeared to be Lazarevic's calling card, but no one was willing to chance it.

We headed south to Austin, Texas, as Amy won the debate with Alistair on where to try next. If Austin turned out like Goshen and Kansas City, we would appease Alistair's hankering to visit New Orleans.

Austin was great for Amy, as her brother, Jeremy Golden Eagle, presently resided there. His large bungalow offered plenty of room to keep us from negatively impacting one another's personal space. Not to mention, the restaurants and nightlife in Austin are exceptional.

We stayed with Jeremy almost a month, and began looking for several houses in the area to comfortably appease everyone. Perhaps that was the problem. We were becoming too much at home. In reality and later in retrospect, we hadn't found a haven of any kind, only distractions from the malevolent unseen eyes of our Hungarian adversary. I could feel him. Roderick felt him, too. Lazarevic, or his spying essence, was somewhere close.

When Beatrice began spending much of her days frowning while warily looking around, Roderick and I overruled Amy's reluctance to leave. She couldn't sense the danger, which surprised me. Even Alistair went out of his way to ensure the blinds and curtains throughout the main floor of Jeremy's place were closed throughout the day, and the doors and windows locked tight each evening.

The uneasiness intensified during our last week in Austin.

"So, can we now go to Nola, Pops?" asked Alistair, a twinkle of orneriness in his soft brown eyes. He had recently completed his regression from a sixty-year-old man to twenty-one. His eyes and generous smile were all that remained as physical traits of the old Georgetown professor, thanks to the 'age reducing' crystals he, Amy, and Beatrice possessed from Iran's Tree of Life.

"Nola?"

"It's how the locals down in Louisiana refer to their wonderful port, William," said Roderick, pulling back the blinds covering the main picture window in Jeremy's living room to peer outside. "It has changed quite a bit since the last time you were there… 1929?"

He chuckled, closing the blinds and joining Cedric near the small wet bar that had become our favored oasis. Roderick seemed almost comfortable in the snakeskin boots and black Stetson he had adopted as his 'new look'—even with his near seven-foot height. A pair of mirrored sunglasses made him appear more Texas Marshall than oil tycoon. Especially with his closely cropped white hair died brown, and the latest cosmetic bronzing upon his ashen skin. Knowing he would soon discard his new get-up for something else, I hadn't needled him about it.

Everyone's emotions remained on edge, wondering when Lazarevic would strike next. Whether the next visit would bring him to us in the flesh.

"I had a layover in 1984, on my way to Houston," I corrected him. "My stay lasted for only three and a half hours, and I never left the airport. So, technically you are correct. But, you know my aversion to most acronyms."

"So, based on some silly prejudice, you'll stall us from making the trip?"

The twinkle had kindled a blaze in Alistair's eyes. Baiting me. Baiting his father to come clean on why I was hesitant about New Orleans. Since we share the same inquisitive trait, I could easily sidestep the interrogation soon to follow his initial question.

"No. Not prejudice. Just the 'still small voice within us all' telling me to keep my eyes peeled," I replied. "And, to not ignore my gut."

"What in the hell, Pops?!"

"I think your dad is picking up the same thing I am," Roderick said to Alistair. "We're running out of time to be willy-nilly in our search for a suitable refuge. Krontos is toying with us. I would rather be someplace that provided a chance to keep surprises to a minimum. I don't think it will happen in a city that invites decadence... do you?"

"What about the Garden District?" Cedric interjected. "And not every place near downtown is for the sinners of the world." He smiled warmly, and his brown eyes were aglow within his smooth ebony complexion. They bore almost the same impish glint that was once his trademark before his sabbatical in Bolivia. He had yet to recover from time spent in another dimension barely tied to the Bolivian and Peruvian worlds most of us understand.

"A better question is '*Where* in the Garden District?'" I moved to squash the debate. "Unless you come from old, connected money, you'd be hard pressed to find something any more suitable than our present location."

"Exactly Amy's point for staying here."

"Which we can't do—unless we're content to be sitting ducks!" Roderick's irritation slipped through his placid veneer as he addressed my son. "You and your bride-to-be need to trust me—as do you *all*—both for my warnings about staying here or heading down to New Orleans. They are both bad ideas! Krontos Lazarevic *is* coming for us—it's only a matter of *when*, and not *if*. He knows we are here… hiding from him. We need to leave within a fortnight, and when we do, we'll need to forget about this place and its comforts. Forget about it all forever. And, make sure we stay open to the sanctuary I know in my heart is out there waiting for us… provided we are diligent in finding it."

Roderick's rebuke hit us all, and in truth was directed mostly toward Amy—who wasn't there at the moment. She and Beatrice had gone out to get their hair done that afternoon. Having to tell my beloved wife and our future daughter-in-law we would be packing up and moving again in the next few days fell on my shoulders.

I expected the worse reaction to come from Amy, whose reluctance to leave her brother behind—her last living relative on Earth—was completely understandable. But it was Beatrice who broke down crying, falling to her knees as tears streamed down her face. My heart felt like it was torn asunder within my chest. I ran to her, gently taking her into my arms as my wife, yes, but also as if she were my child. The heartrending wails were a combination of all she had endured since rejoining my life, along with the rejuvenation that had sped up during the past few months.

When I concluded the story now known as *Immortal Dragon*, Beatrice was pushing thirty-eight—on the downside of that number, and getting younger by the month. Since then, however, changes once noticeable every three to four weeks began taking place in a matter of ten to twelve days. An entire decade disappeared in a matter of two months, and now no one would ever believe Beatrice Barrow was a day over thirty, with some compliments in the twenty-six to twenty-seven year range.

Counting the age reduction Cedric enjoyed from his time with the Yitari people in Paititi—the mystical land invisible on our plane, but until recently a vibrant globe metropolis floating above Lake Titicaca—I was now the oldest in appearance among our group of human misfits. Perpetually thirty despite working on my third millennium, being the father figure in physical terms brought a new perspective.

"There, there, my love… it *will* be all right—everything will be fine," I whispered to her, gently brushing strands of strawberry blonde hair away from the tears, knowing she would be further upset if the stylist's efforts became matted. "Trust me."

She looked into my face, her gorgeous emerald eyes boring into mine. Never before had I seen her this vulnerable… so terribly frightened. Did she feel it, too?

The prickly, invisible voyeur touch of Krontos Lazarevic…. May The Almighty condemn the sick bastard to the very fires of hell!

Yes, I thought it. If only I believed in such a place. Surely the Lord has ways of dealing with all human shortcomings, as evidenced by my perpetual presence in the flesh, no less. Eternal hell defies the idea of a merciful God. Mankind's justice in its primitive form is the only thing calling for endless suffering and excessive retribution. But I digress.

Beatrice recovered, and more quickly than I began to believe might happen. Somewhere inside her, I suppose, remained the resilient ninety-year-old woman I almost lost three years ago. As for Amy, she handled the news stoically, staring ahead with her usually intense green eyes devoid of emotion. Her only acknowledgement was a slight nod, as she swept her long dark hair away from her face. As if she knew sooner or later her protests would become irrelevant in deciding where fate should take us next.

We left on the second Tuesday of August, and to my surprise, my three amigos—Roderick, Alistair, and Cedric—deferred to my choice. Really, it was a process of elimination in my mind, and I was content to travel to any place from Missoula to Yuma. Just as long as the journey took us westward. My only qualms were to avoid the coast, since something about being on the western outskirts of the continent made me uneasy.

But what the guys wanted was specifically the place I had spoken of on several occasions. A town that fascinated me for its unique 'feel'. It had done so since my return to America from England in 1889 with Roderick.

Sedona. Sedona, Arizona.

The name admittedly has a ring to it. My initial suspicions as to why the guys were all in favor of it had more to do with something silly like that. Or, the fact Cedric and Alistair expressed interest in gaining insights from the mass of mediums and psychics who call Sedona home.

But, when Beatrice and Amy expressed similar interest in at least visiting the town that had grown to be a modest city in size, I took it as a positive sign. Like fate was pulling us there next.

We arrived Friday morning, just three days after leaving Austin. Despite being mid-August in the arid portion of America, Sedona immediately reminded Roderick of the Mediterranean climate he had greatly loved and missed terribly. After the death of his wife and child, he rarely returned to that region of the world. I always felt if he could find a similar place far away from so much pain for him, he would settle there. Truly, if Sedona had been where the colonies began, it isn't a far stretch to think the United States capital would be in Arizona, instead of resting between Virginia and Maryland.

"I read online that in the fall the days are typically in the high seventies and the nights drop down to the low fifties—without the humidity we're used to," said Beatrice, noting the fascinated expression and first real smile we had seen on Roderick's face since leaving Abingdon in June. "It's hot today… the temperature on the First Bank sign we passed said ninety-three degrees. But it still feels better than the eighty degree days we'd get in D.C."

Watching her nod thoughtfully, I could tell she was just as impressed as he. She pictured herself living there, as I could see it in her eyes. So far, her impressions were favorable.

Cedric seemed happy with the decision as well. He watched the progress of two men, dressed similarly to how he had re-entered our lives in June, wearing dark robes and matching fezzes on their heads. I teased him about regrets in returning to western customs, since he was dressed in his favored jeans and polo shirt.

"Nah, it's just nice to know I can go back to that here, if I'd like. Provided I don't have to take any bullshit from you or Roderick about it." He laughed.

"I think we can all be happy here," I said, chuckling along with him. "Happier here than anywhere else, I believe."

My words proved prophetic. For the next two months, more and more fortuitous moments happened—enough to where even Amy and Alistair grew grateful for the decision to come to Sedona. They quickly fell in love with the place. In fact, they were the ones who discovered a small ranch just outside of town that we purchased in September. Amy had long been fond of horses, and in many ways, the ranch seemed to be a dream come true for her. A fulfillment of her parents' ambitions, as she revealed to us. Meanwhile, Alistair's lone desire was to be happy with Amy. The ranch potentially took care of one-third of our group's contentment.

Roderick and I liked the thirty-two acres of seclusion, realistically hoping to avoid mortal nuisances like our CIA cronies, whom we'd just as soon never see or hear from again. Beatrice loved the late-nineteenth century craftsmanship that went into the construction of the main house on the property, which likely ensured her continued happiness. She had spent a great deal of time studying up on the history of Alistair's condo in D.C., and the ranch's history gave her something to look forward to each day.

That left Cedric, who might've missed his big city life. However, once he was introduced to the mystic circuit in the city, he launched himself into a tour of checking out as many mediums, psychics, and Tarot card readers as he could fit into each week from the thousands who came to Sedona to strut their stuff. His was the most worrisome situation among us, as obviously he still struggled in coming to terms with what he experienced in Bolivia.

Immortal Tyranny

Having witnessed the violent overthrow of a nation that had survived for many hundreds—if not thousands—of years, did he suffer from a malady akin to post war traumatic syndrome? I worried he did, wondering if someday he'd prove to be a liability when our inevitable face-to-face confrontation with Lazarevic took place.

"Leave him to the soothsayers and witches, Judas," Roderick told me one afternoon, as we watched him leave by taxi for his latest foray into understanding the unknown. "Perhaps there will be enough time for his perspective to click back in place."

"You think it will be that simple?"

"Maybe."

"You know what it could mean if he cracks and we're in a heated confrontation with the Hungarian?"

Roderick chuckled, but it wasn't from amusement. "Let's pray it doesn't come to that."

It did seem best to focus on the things we could control, though I worried a confrontation between us and Cedric was on the horizon. Admittedly, Sedona seemed to have an inordinate amount of self-described mystics. Whereas Cedric approached the scene as a prospector panning for gold, Roderick believed the 'new thinking trends' were horseshit and magnets for all kinds of skullduggery.

It brought to mind a recent conversation I had with Cedric, where I pressed him for details concerning the terrible fall of Patiti. "You don't want to know, William," he advised, the light in his eyes dimming. "Lebanon, Croatia, Afghanistan… were nothing compared to watching hordes of demons—creatures all of us would deem as pure fantasy—tear human beings from limb to limb, and devour them like you and I once tore through a double order of crab legs at Joe's back in the day. Even seeing the agency photographs of Darfur can't compare to seeing a city of millions decimated so brutally. Harvested like cattle moving through a slaughterhouse."

He didn't need to go on to make his point, and I nodded thoughtfully while watching him blow imaginary smoke rings above our heads. Having given up his beloved slim cigars for nearly a year, could this latest crisis be the incident to break his resolve?

I should've known then my own illusions of escaping recent horrors I witnessed were just as foolhardy. Roderick and I were forced to watch Dracul's bloodlust, leaving fresh images to compound similar events we experienced down through the centuries. Dracul was dead, but the animator behind this monster was alive and well, and biding his time.

When it finally happened, I was surprised by how it hit me. The prolonged tension didn't resolve itself in a sense of relief. Rather, when the familiar token from Krontos Lazaveric appeared on the rustic living room mantel one evening, it brought a feeling of condemnation. Like the final lost appeal of a death row inmate, the mood was somber as Roderick stepped up to the mantel and lifted the object from its perch. A rose, clandestinely delivered exactly ten days before Halloween.

"Hmmm... purple this time," he said softly. "A tribute to his delusion as the sovereign ruler of the physical world?"

"More like arrogant prick!" Alistair seethed. His bravado quickly became muted, and he warily looked around the room while pulling Amy closer.

"Arrogant? Maybe. But that's not the message," I said, moving to Roderick's side to take a closer look. "Purple roses primarily stand for enchantment and the fulfillment of wishes. If I were to hazard a guess, this signals Krontos' determination to obtain the Dragon Coin—what he considers to be *his* prized possession. He will seek to claim it in person soon."

Immortal Tyranny

"I can buy that," Roderick agreed, looking around the room. "Is this it?"

"What? You looking for a note this time?" Cedric seemed annoyed. He had joined us moments before the discovery of the rose, having returned from his latest 'reading'.

"We haven't received any notes as of late," I said, carefully taking the rose from Roderick. "I think we'll remain confined to the same tiresome guessing game. Obviously—"

"Wait! What in the hell?!..." Standing behind the sofa with Amy, Beatrice reached behind her back, as if something had suddenly fallen across her shoulders. She picked up whatever it was from the floor. "Oh, my God—it's from *him!"*

Her hands shook as she held out the aged parchment note enclosed with a wax seal for either Roderick or me to take from her. He beat me to it. After removing the seal he hastily opened the note, while I scanned the ceiling and nearby windows for signs of entry. As usual, there weren't any.

"What's it say?" Amy asked worriedly, while the rest of us gathered around Roderick, jockeying for the best view. He shook his head after unfurling the paper and scanning its content. The rest of us soon mimicked his reaction, with Alistair wearing the biggest frown.

To Judas, Roderick, and those you hold dear,

It is time.

Details pertaining to your fate will arrive in the morning. Make sure all of you are present to receive the next instructions. All prior terms remain in effect.

Cordially,

Krontos Lazarevic

Chapter Two

None of us slept worth a damn that night. But after delivering what little comfort Beatrice would accept, as she lay wide awake in our bedroom worrying about the 'fate' to be delivered by Lazarevic sometime after daybreak, Roderick and I stoked a fire in the living room.

The stacked stone fireplace dominated one wall, and sat opposite an enormous picture window facing a colorful view of red sand bluffs to the east. Our latest refuge was built in 1894, in the style of the old mountain lodges scattered throughout the region. Enormous split beams made from solid pine crisscrossed the tall ceiling and were supported by four forty-foot pine pillars. A second floor open veranda surrounded the living room, and at the moment, a thin stream of light from the lamp on Beatrice's nightstand crept into the darkness outside our upstairs bedroom.

I hoped to rejoin my wife soon, with the intent of trying again to lift the worry from her heart, so she could rest her weary mind. Meanwhile, Roderick and I debated whether or not our nemesis truly wanted the Dragon Coin, or would Krontos demand something else instead? There was enough uncertainty to where I found myself playing the devil's advocate, looking for logical objections as to why he wouldn't want the coin—despite his longstanding familiarity with this particular shekel.

"What good could it possibly do him?" I asked quietly, in hopes Beatrice would either not hear our conversation or choose to ignore us altogether. "Suppose his magic has developed to where he no longer needs any coin to keep it going?"

"What... and that he's been playing us all along?" Roderick's expression revealed the idea was a novel one, and something he hadn't previously considered.

"Well, you must admit it wouldn't be out of the realm of possibility for someone like him. Someone who can sway dimensional reality to fit his whims. Right?"

The volatile swirl of tiny golden flakes within his sky blue irises sped up. That, more than his deepening frown, told me this latest idea could threaten any chance of my rejoining Beatrice in our bed. Since neither Roderick nor I require steady sleep, and we often go days on end without such rest during times of crisis, adding any more fuel to our debate seemed unwise. And I had just done that.

"Not necessarily—and, I'm addressing your latest thought," he said. My turn to frown, since I had let down my mental guard while worrying about the effect of my words. "I had considered Krontos no longer needed anything from anyone to fulfill his wicked schemes. If it's true, then all of us—including the rest of mankind—are completely screwed!"

"Ah, so it would seem," I agreed. "But, the fact he is worried about little ole you and me hiding out in this quaint Arizona town tells me he's not godlike just yet."

Roderick shook his head disgustedly and started to say something, but caught himself.

"What is it, Rod? You've been acting like you want to tell me something important for days—long before this latest incident."

True. Actually, I noticed the silent burden he carried nearly a week ago. I had hoped he would reveal his secret naturally, and decided to wait it out. If not for the dreaded token from Lazarevic, I had already planned to broach the matter by this coming weekend.

"I know if pressed to do so, you would relinquish Dracul's coin to his master," he said, shifting in his seat to better regard me. "It may come to that, old friend. I pray it does not, but there are no guarantees of success in protecting all of us from harm, as you know. What are you planning to do if Krontos demands this coin?"

"To save you, my beloved family, and Cedric? I would give him what he wants," I said. "But, what would such a move cost me personally? Since I've never been in a situation like this before, that answer is unknown. You and I will be traveling through uncharted territory. Yet, having said that, reintroducing my cured coins into the world would certainly spell untold disaster. My gut tells me the consequences and curses would be much more severe the next go round."

"So, you'd rather not give your coins in exchange for others. Correct?"

"Yes... but why does any of this matter right now? My brother, I know you so well. Tell me what's up."

I could have, and perhaps should have, made him blurt out the piece he was hiding from me days ago. I prayed my perturbed expression would be enough to get him to come clean.

"I heard from Jeffrey the other day. Jeffrey Holmes? You remember him, don't you?"

"The kid from Buffalo, New York?"

Immortal Tyranny

"Yes. But he's not a kid anymore, having recently celebrated his forty-first birthday," Roderick advised. "Though it was unfortunate he learned your identity from Michael some years back, he has proven to be a good 'silent' fan of yours, Judas. Remember, he's the one who tracked down the Damascus coin before it suddenly disappeared again."

"What a surprise," I deadpanned.

"I'm serious, man!"

We had been sitting at a small dinette near the fireplace, and Roderick stood to tend to the dying flames.

"What if I were to tell you that Jeffrey has found links to a black market deal coming up soon for another coin of yours both of us assumed might never see the light of day for centuries?"

"I'd say better get the damned thing before you blink, or 'poof' it'll be gone!"

"Very funny, smartass," he said, scowling at me as he laid a medium sized log on top of the hearth. A bed of fiery coals from the previous log ignited the new offering. Roderick brushed off his hands and returned to me. "The coin is quite unique and is said to have more mystical properties than your Dragon Coin. It remained for centuries in the possession of a wealthy Jewish family in Poland. No one has seen it since World War II."

"Wait a moment... you can't be serious?" I couldn't believe my ears, and felt like an idiot for playing him as I had. Then again, he didn't need to be so coy. "The Stutthof-Auschwitz coin?"

"Yes, the very one that began the legend of healing among the condemned Jews in the Stutthof concentration camp. It later caused much more excitement —enough to where the coin was eventually discovered in Auschwitz, and then confiscated by the Nazis," Roderick confirmed. He smiled, obviously pleased by my response. "If you'll recall our previous conversation on the subject—and granted it's been some years, now—unlike the other coins, this coin came to Stutthof from a Polish Jewish clan. The Nazis somehow missed it. The coin kept this family safe from harm's way for nearly three months, until the evil of Hitler's Final Solution was too much to defeat.

"The family was separated, and the parents were sent with the oldest brother to Auschwitz. The son, named Simon Lieberman, carried the coin. Legend has it the Nazis missed it again—despite thorough searches and nary a place to hide a coin. Perhaps it was stored in an orifice… in the mouth or anus seems most likely. Anyway, the coin carried mysterious healing powers, as you know. A handful of survivors from these horrific death camps spoke of a magical coin that could heal, somehow feed, and protect dozens from the beatings, random shootings, fateful trips to the gas chambers, etc. They all say it glowed with a blue sheen—the same thing you and I can see in the other coins."

I clearly pictured the excitement I felt about this coin, back when the Second World War ravished Europe and raged through the Pacific islands. Not much reached the United States from our European brothers and sisters until we were fully engaged in war as a nation. Secrets withheld from the general populace, along with whispers of atrocities that scarcely seemed real to those who had never seen such events firsthand, began seeping into America's awareness. Of course, for me it was maddening, as I had known what was happening since September 1939. I desperately wanted to return to Europe in hopes I could save as many of my Jewish brethren as possible. I knew it would be a small amount in comparison to the eventual hundreds of thousands being put to death each month in 1943 and beyond. But it wasn't until I feared the extinction of the bloodlines rooted in Israel that I took matters into my own hands.

This resolve initially hit me full force in the spring of 1944. The other thing to sway me was the rumor of a blood coin in its active state—a true rarity in the twentieth century, since most often I found them in moments of dormancy. Not to mention, the coin that had circulated through two Polish concentration camps was creating hope for the Jewish nation, instead of the usual calamities my coins bring.

Getting an officer commission wasn't as easy for me as some might think. This was before the formation of the CIA, which didn't become active until 1947. I was working in the higher circles of the FBI at the time, and was viewed as a curious dinosaur who somehow looked much younger than I was. After all, the BOI had been absorbed by the newly formed FBI in 1933.

I won't bore everyone with the details. Suffice it to say it took me calling in a favor with Virginia Senator W. Chapman Revercomb to obtain a European field commission. I was stationed in France as a US Army captain by the fall of 1944, and had hoped to slip away to Poland long enough to find my coin and save as many prisoners as possible. But getting away from France proved arduous at best, once the fortunes of the war swung in favor of the allied forces. As the intelligence photographs from the death camps began to reach my contacts in Washington the following January, I realized it was too late for me to do anything.

The greatest atrocity known to modern man was nearing its conclusion and would soon be revealed for the diabolical horror it was. And the coin? The Nazis had recovered it by then. My same contacts in Washington talked about some excitement over a recently discovered small item that was hailed as "the greatest occult relic in possession of the Third

Reich." I clearly recall how my heart froze upon hearing this news. It was never The Almighty's plan for the Germans to possess this coin.

"Judas. Judas.... Hey, man are you all right?"

"Huh? Oh, shit. Sorry about that, Rod." I must've looked like a total ass, staring out into space while missing nearly everything Roderick said. "I got caught up in a moment of nostalgia."

"And you missed every damned word I said!" he chided. "Tell you what.... Let's talk about this more when the sun comes up and we can work on a plan of attack as a group."

"Attack? I'm not liking the sound of that word," I said, although the prospects of me holding my wife close in the hours before dawn suddenly improved. "Why don't we do the corporate thing and label it as a 'call to action meeting' instead?"

"Semantics."

"Hey, I'm a little sensitive right now."

I winked and he chuckled, shaking his head.

"Sleep on it... if you can, Judas." Roderick stood, dampened the fire, and made his way toward the lone bedroom on the main floor, which belonged to him.

I waited until he disappeared down the hall before I headed upstairs. Convinced nearly everyone else remained awake, I removed my shoes and consciously pulled my aura in, praying if anyone sensed my approach, it would only be Beatrice.

Fantasies entered my thoughts of what passion could bring if my cherished wife was game for something beyond mere comfort. But as I quietly pushed open our bedroom door, her soft snores confirmed this was neither the time nor place for lovemaking.

I smiled lovingly at Beatrice, passed out with the television remote held loosely in her fingertips. I gently removed it,

Immortal Tyranny

turned off the TV, and carefully wrapped her body in her favorite blanket. She smiled as I climbed into bed next to her, drawing close. Then I patiently waited for dawn and its promise of warmth and light to arrive, and whatever Krontos Lazarevic had in store for us.

Chapter Three

"Why can't Krontos just stop by and pick up the damned thing?" lamented Alistair. "And, why in the hell does he want us to meet his cronies in New York?"

Early afternoon. We had recently received the promised correspondence from Lazarevic. While his previous note was bathed in thinly veiled hostility, the latest correspondence was a sterile affair. No *rosa sericea* accompanied the delivery, and the priority mail envelope came with an actual physical address: The Ritz-Carlton in New York City. Did Krontos presently reside there? Maybe... or maybe not. Enclosed with an impersonal note were six first class airline tickets and two reserved suites at the same establishment.

"Well, Ali, at least you won't have to wait long for answers to those questions. According to the tickets our assigned United flight leaves just after nine o'clock in the morning," I said, looking for levity. I laid the tickets face-up in the middle of the dining room table, where everyone had gathered. "The note says a limousine will be waiting for us at LaGuardia Airport, and will bring us to the hotel. If he's there, you'll have your answers by mid-afternoon, I'd guess."

"And, if this is just a wild goose chase, and we never get to meet the guy?"

"Then you get the satisfaction in knowing you were right." I replied, shooting him a perturbed look. "But approaching a solution from a gloomy point of view will only ensure things turn out badly."

My son has always been a stick in the mud, so to speak. But, I didn't realize the physical aspects of growing older are what had mellowed him in his former 'normal' life. I am admittedly dismayed the restoration to full youth has created a petulant ass for the most part. I hold out hope someday this prevalent attitude breaks like a fever. It's Roderick's prophecy for my boy, and I pray it happens sooner than later.

He shrugged indifferently, and Amy went to work on comforting him, rubbing his shoulders affectionately. In all honesty, I'm more prone these days to cut him slack in most instances of surliness—especially after Krontos' lightly veiled threats in the letter he left for us in Abingdon in June: *Your loved ones will summarily be returned to Dracul's menu.* The vampire is dead forever, but does this mean Krontos shares his cannibalistic tendencies? Roderick and I witnessed the rampant bloodshed Dracul indulged himself in, feasting on human organs and muscle in addition to human plasma.

"We mustn't give in to the thought patterns being fed to us," Roderick advised. I turned my attention to him and he nodded. "Yes, I am addressing you, William."

"What in the hell?" Cedric snickered, and shook his head. He looked almost amused, which certainly meant he wasn't. "Do you two ever think you'll tire of the covert messages you send back and forth?"

"How to change nineteen hundred years of annoyance? Is that what you're asking?" Maybe it would have been prudent to ignore the dig, yet I felt compelled to respond. Not only that, but also the urge to lecture this relative youngster, since Cedric was in his early sixties. In truth, the only person with less years here was Amy. "The answer should be obvious—"

"Judas! *Shhh!*" Roderick slammed a palm onto the table, catching everyone off guard. He held us all in a sullen gaze before continuing. "How do you think a master sorcerer can alter dimensional reality to where the vast majority of people are unaware it's happening? I tell you it has everything to do with the basic premises of metaphysics. And what do we know is a key ingredient?"

His voice surrounded us, which added eerie urgency to his questions. Questions made worse since they were directed at me. Perhaps justifiably so, as I knew exactly what he was getting at.

"Our thoughts and perceptions are in part holding our reality together," I said, hating how this sounded like the dialogue in a religious thriller novel, where one character would ask another character an obvious, though awkward, question to move the plot along. Or, worse, like Bob Barker and Rod Roddy years ago—"Tell us what they've won, Rod." "Well, Bob… it's a new car!"

"Exactly," said Roderick, without smugness. He hated this, too. "For everyone else's benefit, I tell you all to question anything that feels unnatural in your mind. This includes behavior tendencies you actually have that suddenly feel exaggerated. The energy around us has been agitated for more than a week, and I believe our increased bickering is partly due to this. Though impossible to prove, I'd bet everything I'm worth Krontos has been playing us in this manner ever since we left Abingdon. If you'll think about it, every one of our moves during the past four months has been preceded by heightened tension like we're dealing with at present."

The proverbial feather hitting the floor would be apropos to describe the dumbfounded looks and silence as we all considered the truth of Roderick's observation.

"What we must never lose sight of is the diabolical nature of our adversary," he continued. "Krontos' motives are always harmful to the human race. You've heard it said before that madmen revel in the world burning to ashes around them. That image defines him better than anything else. Especially, since he prefers to employ his destructive influences behind the scenes."

"So, does it mean we're like some dumbass sheep, as we prepare to fly out to meet this jerkoff?" asked Cedric. Surely this was another moment where he wished things had worked out better in Paititi. "Roderick and William... you two should know better, in dealing with someone like this. It's a no-win situation, and it can only end one way. *Badly!*"

"While it's true it does seem hopeless—at least at first glance—William and I have been discussing some options that might work in our favor," Roderick advised. He motioned for the guys to join the ladies, who had already sat down at the table. "I ask that you keep your minds open as we discuss an alternative buy-out plan."

"Buy out plan? Sounds like we're trying to avoid a hostile takeover," Amy observed, grimacing as if this notion brought unpleasant memories from her former life as a successful corporate attorney.

Her deep green eyes were on fire, as were Beatrice's. The pair reminded me of hungry felines with matching gazes, one brunette and the other with lustrous locks the angry color of the Scots. Much of what was to be discussed would strike many as whimsical bullshit. I prayed they kept their mental channels open long enough to absorb most of what was coming. Lord knew it might save their lives as we invaded the world of

Krontos Lazarevic. It had become obvious to Roderick and me that we had no choice other than taking the game to our menace, instead of waiting for what would come next. We intended to step up the aggression once we made contact, which now had been set to happen the next day.

"Like the small companies in the business world desperate to hold on to their individuality—their identity—yes, our battle is quite similar," said Roderick, after he sat down with the rest of us. "Here's the wild card we intend to play. We know Krontos wants the Dragon Coin. But to give it to him may bring terrible consequences, both to us personally and to the world in general. So, we will seek to stall him while we make arrangements to purchase another coin that might suit Krontos better."

"What coin? A *blood* coin? Nobody told me anything about new coins." Alistair glared at me accusingly.

"I just found out early this morning, Ali. Although, it is a coin I've known about for some time," I said, meeting his gaze without relenting. It wasn't hard to picture delivering an overdue butt paddling to my kid, and I hoped my eyes carried enough cobalt anger to subdue the fiery glint in his. "It's one that disappeared from my awareness more than a thousand years ago, carried in secret by a Russian Jewish family that eventually relocated to Poland. After they were incarcerated by the Nazis in World War II, the coin became legendary among Jewish survivors of Stutthof and Auschwitz concentration camps."

"No shit, huh?" said Cedric, nodding thoughtfully. "So, what kept you from collecting it before now?"

"The Nazis eventually learned of its presence in Auschwitz," said Roderick. "They killed everyone associated with the coin… or so they thought. Several former Auschwitz inmates spoke of the coin after they received nourishment and

Immortal Tyranny

recovered enough stamina to discuss the horrors they endured. Yes, William, I knew about this, too."

He cut me a look begging me not to grill him on how he knew these details. I assumed he might've had a cursory knowledge fed by Jeffrey's detailed report from a week ago. Obviously, not so.

"No one believed them," I said, recalling those interviews.

The allied teams of physicians and psychiatrists managed to dam the stream of information about the coin soon after the war ended. By December 1945 all mention of the coin was lost, either by threats of prolonged detention or effective drugs to those who refused to 'give up delusions and face reality'. Sadly, I believed the information might be lost forever, as the only surviving account of the coin came from Sophi Lieberman, who successfully posed as a Stutthof camp employee and escaped being shipped to Auschwitz with her parents and older brother. Her account was duly recorded and saved by two nuns who sheltered her in the basement of a Catholic church in Danzing.

"Maybe I missed something," said Beatrice, pausing to clear her throat as if she hadn't intended to join the conversation. "I understand this poor family lost the coin to the Nazis, and I assume it must have moved from them to someone else. How do you intend to get it now?"

"The coin has recently resurfaced via the antiquities black market," Roderick advised. "An old friend of ours in the CIA, Jeffrey Holmes, brought it to my attention a little over a week ago."

"The kid from Buffalo?" asked Cedric.

"Yes, that *kid.*" I smiled at Roderick, since I wasn't the only one who failed to update their age perception of Agent Holmes.

"How will the bidding for it work?" Beatrice persisted. "I presume you are planning to buy it sight unseen. What if it's a fraud?"

Good question, and one I hadn't seriously considered. But Roderick had.

"Jeffrey utilized resources that could potentially get him fired if the agency ever found out he put them to use for this," said Roderick. "The coin is the veritable real deal, and comes with letters attributed to Dr. Joseph Mengele and the last two commandants of Auschwitz, Arthur Liebehenschel and Richard Baer. There is also a small journal included in the auction offering that belonged to Heinrich Himmler, and examines the supernatural aspects of the coin discovered by the Nazis toward the end of 1944."

"Sheesh, there's no telling how much this will go for."

Beatrice eyed me worriedly after she said this, slowly shaking her head. Did I ever mention I'm not a fan of a woman's intuition, when it could potentially invite thunderclouds to come our way?

"The opening bid is six million euros—which is beyond absurd for a silver shekel," said Roderick. "But I expect it to go for at least twice that much, which might cause a temporary hole in our finances, eh William?"

"That's only if we can't get Krontos to go after it himself, and leave us out of this mess," I said, grimacing as I briefly considered the myriad ways this could turn out adversely for us. So many things could go wrong, and the limited list of things going our way was shrinking. "That would be ideal. But, if he insists on taking the Dragon Coin, us having the 'Stutthof-Auschwitz' coin to make up for it might counteract the consequences. Hopefully it would stem the cost of losing a cured coin to someone as evil as Lazarevic."

Immortal Tyranny

The mood at the table became reflective and dark, and Roderick and I exchanged one more knowing glance that seemed to irritate everyone else. But other than mutterings from Alistair and a heavy sigh from the ladies, Roderick's and my agreement to curtail the conversation in favor of picking up Angus steaks for dinner proved to be an effective distraction.

I believe we all knew there was little to fret about until we arrived in New York the next day. Until then, our adversary held all of the cards. Whether he accepted our counter offer of another coin would determine our next move as a group. Other than affirming and reaffirming this information with our four mortal companions, the subject soon turned to what to pack for the trip, making sure each of us brought enough warm clothes for autumn in New York City.

We retired to our rooms by ten o'clock, hoping to get enough rest for our 9:05 a.m. flight. For the second straight night, I watched my beloved as she slept, hovering protectively as I lay by her side.

It was the only thing to bring me comfort.

Chapter Four

I should have expected someone to throw a wrench into our affairs. Should've been ready for anything. Though we understood much about the fickle and cruel nature of Krontos Lazarevic, we were ill prepared for his latest shenanigans.

"What do you mean he canceled our trip?!"

Roderick flinched as I addressed him, the first clue my tone carried unwarranted irritation toward him. Beatrice dropped her packed carry-on bags near the top of the stairs, gently grasping my arm as I prepared to hurry down to the main floor like an agitated tom turkey. I whirled to meet her pleading gaze.

"Hear the rest of what Roderick has to say before you say anything else," she cautioned, tenderly. "It's not his fault, William."

She reached up and caressed the left side of my face with her free hand. Her touch was cool and comforting. Very few human beings have been able to calm my anger like Beatrice. Only my mother and younger sister, Esther, from my mortal days in Judea could do it. And, admittedly, on occasion Roderick has managed this feat... just not that morning.

Immortal Tyranny

Beatrice tightened her grip on my arm until I nodded my consent to her admonishment. She smiled lovingly and I allowed the grin that often turns into a smirk to shine through.

Hey, it was a start.

We strode downstairs together, making my pace less resolute than it might've been. Everyone else stood in the kitchen, apparently waiting on us to emerge from our bedroom suite. The clock above the mantel gave the local time as 6:52 a.m. Several suitcases sat next to the fireplace, apparently left there when Roderick gave his initial update.

"When I prepared to call the limousine service to ensure our car was on the way, I happened to see this latest note waiting outside the back patio door." He held out a folded-over parchment, familiar as Krontos' favored medium. My buddy motioned for me to take it once we joined him and the others in the kitchen. "Go ahead, take it."

Roderick cast a grateful glance to my better half for her nudge to my ribs. I offered him a muted apology as I took the letter.

Roderick and Judas,

I have decided to wait on our meeting. As such, please consider this an indefinite reprieve. Should I determine a need for the Dragon Coin, I will contact you expediently.

In the meantime, enjoy your freedom in Sedona. But stay close to your ranch, in the event your presence here is required. Your indentured status, and that of your loved ones, remains in effect.

Sincerely,

Immortal Tyranny

Krontos

"So, we are casual acquaintances now?" I mused, chuckling at the irony. Compared to the normal detached coolness we had become accustomed to from our invisible overlord, this latest correspondence was almost merry in comparison. "Next thing you know we'll be getting a Christmas card from the bastard."

"Since he has a penchant for delivering his messages without warning, I suggest we keep the derogative responses to a minimum," chided Roderick, mindful to keep his tone as sweet as Beatrice's had been just minutes earlier. "We would do well to speak of him respectfully."

"Personally, I prefer Pops' response," said Alistair, absently twirling fingers through his long, dark bangs that had grown unchecked since my last update. "After all, being an indentured servant isn't exactly a title to be proud of."

"So, you showed everyone else this letter, I take it?" I asked, trading impish glances with my boy. As for my dig about the letter's privacy, I preferred to not divulge much information from the Hungarian devil—especially anything addressed specifically to Roderick and me.

"I gave them the general gist," said Roderick, eyeing me seriously. "They have a right to know what we're up against."

"And, my money's on this cat Krontos gaining an edge from what we discussed last night, William," said Cedric. Dressed in a sharp black polo shirt and slacks, his hands fidgeted as if the longing for his slim panatelas had grown tenfold since our last private conversation. Lots of nervous energy going on around here. "You've got to admit it makes the most sense for an abrupt turnabout like this."

Immortal Tyranny

It did make sense... perfectly. It also meant we were far behind Krontos' next move. If the mention of the Stutthof-Auschwitz coin was behind our adversary's sudden change of heart, then he had far bigger fish to fry than merely aborting our travel plans for his sadistic pleasure.

"We need to get to the coin before Krontos does," I said, directing my words to Roderick. "Who do we—"

"I'm already on it, William," he said, interrupting me. "I've been on the phone twice in the last hour with Bennevento in Rome. I had a hunch the asking price for the coin would skyrocket if Krontos became a player in the stakes. And, he definitely has joined the early bids. But the amount the new entry point has risen to now means we need assistance in covering the coin's cost, until we can access our Swiss reserves."

Shit!

For those unfamiliar, Bennevento Vitorio is an alchemist friend who long ago betrayed us. Remorseful for his shortcomings against Roderick and me, Bennevento has spent the past five centuries trying to make amends.

"How high is the price?" I asked.

"Just shy of eleven million euros," Roderick replied.

"According to what you told me the other night, the official auction is scheduled for Halloween—one week from tomorrow," I said, feeling a renewed surge of anger rising within. "If the cost is skyrocketing now, how in the hell will it be affordable at all by then? It isn't worth losing everything to get it—especially, when The Almighty seems ready for me to retrieve a coin, He clears a path and aligns events to make it happen. I've never had to mortgage the farm to help Him out."

"It's not always so easy," countered Roderick, motioning for everyone to either move into the dining room or living area. A sure sign this was going to be a drawn-out discussion.

"Lately, it hasn't been that clean. Not to mention, collecting coins with you has become a hazardous and often deadly business."

"Why don't you two just let Krontos purchase the coin unhindered and call it a day?" Alistair suggested, grimacing disgustedly. Another sign his perspective from three years ago had dramatically changed. "You can try again for it in twenty years, when you've got nothing better to do to appease your wanderlust."

"If only it were that easy, son," I told him. "Twenty years could easily become three to four centuries, if we're not careful. And, although I'd like to think that you, Amy, and your mother would still be with us in four hundred years, none of you are truly immortal. The chances of avoiding serious injury between now and then will become less favorable as the centuries march on. Not to mention, Almighty God might not look kindly on me deviating from the path I started taking seriously forty years ago with you, Ali."

Alistair nodded thoughtfully, and I worried I might've offended him and Amy, as well as Beatrice. Their expressions matched his, and I would have to wait to revisit this reaction with my wife later on.

"Why don't the rest of you go into town and get some donuts or something for breakfast, while William and I come up with a plan?" Roderick clapped his hands, as if this would help shoo the rest of our group out the front door.

"I'd rather wait until I find out what mischief you two will get us into, if you don't mind," said Alistair. "I'd bet Cedric, Amy, and Mom would rather stay, too."

Roderick tried to coax them out the door again, but it quickly became obvious we'd get nothing done until we relented. With a promise to stop within the next hour for breakfast, the group moved into the living room.

Immortal Tyranny

"Okay... I will spell it out clearly for everyone," Roderick advised, as he stood in front of the fireplace, which provided the best vantage point to view everyone else. I shared the loveseat with Beatrice and the rest of our group sat on the sofa. "Benevento Vitorio is an immortal friend of William's and mine. An alchemist who has had close ties to The Vatican for centuries, he frequently provides access to information we could never obtain from anywhere else. He was instrumental in helping us deal with Viktor Kaslow down in South America last year. And, as Beatrice, Amy, and Alistair are aware, Benevento helped us in our efforts to track down Dracul and The Dragon Coin."

He waited to go on, perhaps expecting Alistair or Cedric to either pose questions or derisive comments. When neither happened, Roderick continued.

"Some of what I'm about to reveal, I have not had a chance to clear with William first, as you know," he said, pausing to regard me. I nodded for him to go on, while my stomach felt queasy—the sure sign something disagreeable was coming. "Benevento understands the seriousness of what is happening for a number of reasons. Rarely have I found him as thorough and candid as he was this morning during our conversation. It turns out Rome has been watching Krontos for centuries—since the mid-fourteenth century, at least. Krontos has often taken an active, meddling role in the kingdoms of Europe. The evolution and eventual dissolution of governments have long fascinated and attracted him.

"This is important for what he sought to accomplish with his sorcery back in the day, and the continued black magic he dabbles in now to influence the power structure among the Slavic nations, in particular. It is the mafia empire Krontos has controlled since the 1960s that brought the latest warnings to The Vatican about something huge going down in the organization. This news comes from spies loyal to the Holy See, and Benevento advised that the news surrounds the planned restoration of an ancient shrine belonging to Krontos."

Roderick paused to sip the tea he apparently brewed while Beatrice and I were upstairs.

"Ever hear the phrase *Mortis imago Trinitatis argenteum*?"

Our companions unanimously indicated they had not. I, on the other hand, recalled this phrase. But it was the English translation that inspired a chill across my spine.

"The Silver Trinity of Death," I said, hoping Roderick wouldn't mind me translating the phrase for the group. "I've often wondered if this vile shrine actually exists."

"Apparently it does," he said, smiling weakly. This was supposed to be the thing he and I discussed in private, and I hated the information being disseminated to everyone else like this. "Before Krontos reanimated the lifeless corpse of Vlad Tepes, he created the shrine using that coin and two others from you, William, which he procured during his long, natural life. Not long after he stepped into immortality, by way of an elixir not unlike the one the St. Germaine brothers once concocted, he set out to test the legend of the trinity.

"He was not the first to try to create it, but he certainly was the first to succeed. Legends you and I have read about, back when you called yourself Emmanuel, foretell the ability to enforce one's will upon the natural world and its events."

"I remember," I said, and all eyes were upon me, as I erroneously expected to happen earlier when I translated the Latin phrase. "I feel like kicking myself for never suspecting Krontos as the Hungarian that Juan Garia de Moguer mentioned long ago. Do you remember my mention of a mysterious Buda nobleman that Juan had once met, who carried two shekels taken from two Ottoman rulers at their deathbeds?"

"Yes... I believe so," he acknowledged. "Something about both rulers seeking last minute penance to wash away years of bloodshed inspired by the coins."

I had forgotten many of the details, until Roderick mentioned the Ottoman chieftains, renowned for unquenchable bloodshed. Old memories flooded my awareness. Memories of evil men hiding behind the Mohammedan title of *Khalifat Rasul Allah*. Both were instrumental in spreading the influence of Islam, which might've become extinct like so many religions and philosophies have done during my extensive stay on planet Earth, without excessive violence to keep it thriving.

"Anyway, with three blood coins in his possession that once belonged to you, as Judas Iscariot, Krontos Lazarevic was able to explore world domination by means of metaphysical doors and windows—openings that Einstein and others referred to as portals and wormholes. The very things we dealt with recently in Bolivia," Roderick explained. "Why he gave up the third coin to save Vlad and create Dracul has always baffled me, since in effect it limited his freedom outside our normal reality. Granted, he did a number on us all when we traveled to Montenegro this past summer...."

Roderick's voice trailed off, and it appeared he fell into a trance. I managed to catch him before he collapsed.

"Are you all right, Rod?" I asked him, snapping my fingers in front of his eyes. He blinked.

"What happened?"

"We were hoping you could tell us," I said.

"I honestly don't know." He tried to stand straight, but sat down gently in front of the hearth. "I was picturing what Tampara had told me long ago, while you were getting to know the Cherokee nation here in America, around 1470. When I mentioned the tortures you and I endured in Spain being the reason for my delayed return to the land that would eventually become Bolivia, Tampara told me about the diminutive white haired European he would see now and then in the plane that contains the realm of Paititi. Or did, until the war Cedric told us about."

"What did he tell you about Krontos?" I asked. Surely everyone else was just as curious.

Roderick didn't answer right away, and seemed to be listening to a sound or voice undetectable to the rest of us.

"I know why Krontos has changed his mind," he said finally, in a hushed voice. "And, it makes sense why he would want to jam the circuits in my head that brought forth the memory of Tampara. My ancient friend said something about three bands of light that followed the little old man, and Tampara could tell the energy rivaled the purity of the power source enabling Paititi to float above Lake Titicaca, as it did until Cedric watched it collapse in flames into the lake...."

Roderick started to fall asleep, as if whatever force attacking him absorbed his consciousness.

"Rod... *Rod!* Snap out of it!" I shouted.

"Huh?"

His eyes opened, barely. He raised his hands, using his fingers to draw an imaginary line around his head. Then Roderick's eyes opened fully, as his layman's sorcery worked. The swirl of gold flecks glowed eerily within his bright blue irises.

"Are you okay now?" I persisted, hovering above him.

"Yes," he said, looking up at me. "Krontos does not want to deal with the tainted remnants of Vlad Tepes' energy that is forever part of the Dragon Coin. Instead, he is attracted to the purity of the 'Holocaust Coin'. That's the name he has for it."

"What in the hell?"

Immortal Tyranny

Alistair whispered this as he and Amy came over to us, followed by Beatrice. Cedric remained seated, looking even more ready for one of his cherished slim cigars.

"It's tied to what you sensed and have not told us, William," said Roderick, trying to rise to his feet. He fell back down, and I motioned for him to rest until the spell had fully passed. "Krontos is not interested in revenge for Dracul, as we originally surmised, after finding our plundered fortress in Abingdon. He sees us—especially you—as a threat to getting what he wants."

Everyone's focus shifted to me, and frankly, I was at a loss for words. My druid pal had managed to define what I could not. The relentless stream of images, thoughts, and words bombarding my mind these past few months—and that had reached a fevered pitch during the past week—suddenly became clear. Or, the coded message had done so.

"Tell us, Pops... and this time no bullshit."

"Okay," I sighed. "Krontos doesn't want to watch the world burn after all. He simply wants to own it. Completely."

Chapter Five

For three days we sat on pins and needles—largely because Roderick suggested we wait to see if Krontos would contact us. Never mind the fact our discussions continued to revolve around reasons *not* to wait. Not everything that comes to a gifted psychic—even one as old as Roderick—is a true premonition. Sometimes, fear gets in the way. Unless impressions are defined in a calm and peaceful moment, they can easily be misunderstood and ignored. It becomes direly critical to make sure one's panic doesn't obscure or twist a solution into an option that gets avoided.

"The longer we sit around here debating whether or not the coin's price is going to increase or not, the worse our chances become of securing it," I said, wearily. We had turned the dining room into a data center, each of us with laptops, tablets, notepads and pens. Take-out cartons and pizza boxes were piled as several unstable towers in the table's middle. "Jeffrey and Benevento have now confirmed the dealer resides in Berlin, and we know two other bidders have emerged. Correct?

Immortal Tyranny

Didn't you say one is a Saudi Shiek, and the other a collector of Nazi memorabilia in Switzerland?"

"Yes, this is true," confirmed Roderick.

He released a low sigh and eyed me sullenly, as if forced to re-explain his preferred protocol to an imbecile for the umpteenth time. Unlike the mortals in our midst, he and I had avoided rest and consistent meals the past few days. He was running himself ragged, looking for an alternative solution that wasn't there. As much as he dreaded it, risking a direct confrontation with Krontos was necessary in gaining an edge.

"Then let's quit this frigging charade and go to Germany," said Cedric, to which Amy and Alistair agreed heartily. "William made the same suggestion last night, after you, Roderick, gave us the latest info on the coin's price. There must be some other way to snag the sucker before the official auction event takes place. There's still five days to go, and last we heard, the early bid was sitting at eighteen million. It's probably higher now, since we haven't heard a damned thing all day!"

"You still fail to understand what Krontos is capable of doing to *all* of us if we disobey his admonishment to stay here!" said Roderick, angrily. "We need to stay put—right here—until he says otherwise. He will summon us to New York again, or even Europe very soon. I'm *certain* of it."

To Roderick's credit, he was right. Krontos would likely be enraged if we weren't relaxing at our Sedona ranch when he made contact again. But I was surprised to find my druid pal's usual gumption had been sucked dry since the strange experience the other day. Roderick's growing subservience to Krontos made it increasingly clear the sorcerer's subtle attack on Roderick's psyche was successful. My buddy's normally clear perspective on all things had been muddied.

"So, when the auction takes place in five days, you're content to just sit here and bid remotely for the Stutthof-Auschwitz coin? And that's if we can come up with the money," I said. "You sure you're ready to simply take your chances from five thousand miles away?"

"Yes," he said softly, shaking his head as if he understood he couldn't defend his point of view.

"Meanwhile, we have one of the most diabolical minds you and I have ever dealt with—maybe the worst in all of recorded history—residing in New York, or more likely, someplace in Europe." I closed my laptop and notepad, signaling my resignation from the bullshit exercise. "He could very well be in Berlin right now. Do you honestly believe Krontos is going to leave the bidding for the coin to chance?"

"Perhaps not. But if we can't win fairly, he would beat us anyway!"

Roderick's voice shook, and I worried our adversary had tapped into our latest conversation.

"Well, I'm done, too. I guess we should clean up here and pick out a movie to watch tonight," said Alistair, closing his laptop. Amy and Beatrice did the same, and I expected Cedric to soon follow. "Pops, we'll have to see about this coin some other time. Hopefully, it won't be in some twisted new reality created by Krontos."

Well done, my boy!

Roderick continued to type updates into his laptop. But I could tell Alistair's words affected him.

"Is everyone forgetting about the coin photographs and carbon dating reports promised to us from the dealer?" asked Roderick, pleadingly. "We'll have as much information as anyone physically in Berlin will receive. What if we traveled there and the coin turned out to be a fake?"

"All the more reason to give up now and polish up the Dragon Coin for his highness, Krontos Lazarevic," I said, rising from the table. "I'm done, my brother."

"But... but you can't quit. It's your coin, and *your* responsibility!"

I was on my way to the splendid plasma television set, wondering if it was too late to place a friendly wager on the Monday night football contest coming on in twenty minutes. But Roderick's dig could not go unanswered.

"Do you even hear yourself?" I rebuked him, while everyone else began clearing the table. Time to put things back in order. "It is indeed my coin *and* my responsibility, Rod!"

I moved to him and felt overwhelming sadness emanating toward me. He looked up with a bewildered expression, as if he didn't understand why he wasn't allowed to carry out the impulses prompted by something other than his gut. Was it his mind or heart that had been meanly hijacked? Perhaps both?

"I should've done this days ago, and as your friend and eternal companion on this earth, I'm doing it now," I told him. He nodded slightly while his eyes flashed defiantly. But I clearly saw the Roderick of old still in there. "I'm taking over from here on out. Whether you like it or not, we *are* going to Germany, and will leave as soon as I can confirm the arrangements."

I half expected unseen fingers to invade my personal space. Perhaps something like an acute headache, and Krontos would use his voyeuristic talent to probe inside my brain. But nothing happened.

After making sure Beatrice was up to entertaining Alistair and Amy in my absence, I headed for the office Roderick and I shared. Cedric accosted me before I reached my destination, as I thought he might.

"Man, this is almost too damned jacked-up for me to deal with," he said, his left fingers caressing a pencil as if it was the cancer stick he craved. "Just promise me that you won't back down on what you said in there. I remember long ago reading how the Nazi influence in Europe was so gradual the Jews became blind to the encroaching danger—like frogs in warm water that's steadily brought to a boil. Know what I mean, man?"

"Alistair came home with that fun frog fact when he was a young lad in Glasgow," I said, chuckling at how the group's perception of me had gone from bullheaded ass to demure pup, after I allowed Roderick to lead us from Abingdon undeterred. It seemed high time I took the reins again. "Don't worry about me changing my mind, Cedric. Everything points to us going to Germany, and I'd need a damned good reason to abort the idea."

"You're not worried about Krontos carrying out his earlier threats against Beatrice, Alistair, and the rest of us?" His warm brown eyes danced as he studied my facial reaction to his question. There wasn't a reaction... at least not a physical one.

"I was," I admitted. "Until the rose and note shit found its way here. There's no way to protect my beloved wife and son, as well as you and Amy. Besides, the six airline tickets delivered to us the other day confirmed my hunch he views us as one big happy family. Trying to hide any of you from Krontos will do no good, and might make things exponentially worse."

"Good. So, we're definitely traveling with you to Germany. Right?"

"First to New York, and if that goes without a hitch, then yes, we'll be on our way to Berlin," I assured him. "Regardless how this turns out, we're operating as a complete group going forward.

Immortal Tyranny

Cedric nodded. "I'll never forget Paititi, man. Everything seemed perfect until news of the coming war with Bochicha and his son, Hurakan, reached King Bashaan. He dismissed that shit as if it would never get serious enough to worry about," he said, glancing longingly toward the living room where Beatrice, Amy, and Alistair erupted into boisterous laughter. The tension release called to us both... although I needed to take care of our travel arrangements first. "If Krontos is successful in restoring his Silver Trinity of Death, I believe things will go very badly for all of us. Hell, the entire world will be up shit's creek if it comes to that."

Cedric's voice cracked and he looked like he wanted to add something, but grimaced instead. With a nod, he left me to take care of our travel arrangements. I watched him move back down the hall to the living room, where more laughter drifted toward me.

Fun times, though perhaps not for long. My heart ached, as every decision from now until we reached a permanent resolution carried the potential for lasting happiness or perpetual hell. I muttered a prayer from my youth, asking The Almighty for wisdom and His mercy to envelope us all... and to make sure I didn't screw this up.

Chapter Six

"What if we are never here again? What if he wins and we lose?"

Beatrice stood facing the sunset from the open doorway to the cabin at the western edge of the ranch's expanse. Secluded enough to where she could feel comfortable in her negligee, where the sun's dying rays revealed her taut nakedness beneath white satin lace. Sitting on the edge of the bed, I watched goose bumps rise from the evening's coolness seeping in from outside, wrestling with the warm blaze in the nearby fireplace. Or, perhaps her skin's response arose from the mention again of our inevitable face-to-face confrontation with Krontos.

"He won't win—not in the long run," I assured her, coming up close behind. I placed my hands gently around her waist to pull her near. She relaxed against my bare chest, and I kissed her softly on the right side of her neck. A slight groan arose from her throat. "I pray we stop him, but unlike previous excursions, it is my foremost priority to keep all of you safe and sound. Then, when our business is done in Germany—and hopefully we win the coin by bid or some other means—I will bring you back to this wonderful place.... When it's safe enough to be here, of course."

"Hmmm.... I believe you mean it, William," she said, her voice husky as my steady assault of tiny kisses resumed. Her native Scottish brogue comes through strongest when incited by heightened passion, be it sex or anger. "But what... what if he's stronger than you think. He's... he's crafty, and I can tell that from my limited... limited...."

"Limited experience with him?" I finished for her, grinning slyly, though she could only catch a glimpse of the impish glow in my eyes as she glanced back at me. I gently brushed her loosened locks aside so she could better see me. "Am I distracting you?"

"You could say that." She moaned, and tried to turn and face me. But I wasn't done with her neck yet... time to move on to the other side. "What are you doing to me, my love?"

"Would you like for me to stop?"

"No... no, I don't."

"Good, then I'll continue." I moved up to her left ear, gently nibbling on the back of it."

"Oh, my God... you are such a *scoundrel* sometimes, William!"

"You know... if I truly was a lesser man, and wanted to take advantage of you right now, I could damn near hypnotize you simply by seduction, and allay all your fears until we safely returned home," I said, glancing in the mirror beside the door. Despite all we had been through lately, the virile intensity in my deep blue eyes remained, surely inspired by my wife's closeness. "What do you think of that?"

"Ah… ahh… I think…. I think it's bullshit, William."

And just like that, she was out of my sensual charms and whirling around to face me directly.

"Well, that was fun while it lasted," I said, wearing the smirk she adores almost as much as she loathes.

"You can pick up where you left off in a moment," she said, holding me in her fiery gaze. Her emerald eyes burned easily through all my defenses, and now I was the sexually disadvantaged prey. The tables had turned in an instant. "But first, I want the truth about everything we can expect. No bullshit, darling."

She brushed her hand against my chest, and a rush of tingles swept through me. I daresay had she threatened to tear my fingernails and eyelashes off one by one, as they used to do in Cambodia forty years ago, she wouldn't have gotten as far as she did with those eyes boring into me. It was as if she could literally see inside my very soul.

"I think I need to sit down." Truly, I did. Her heat was intoxicating, and I wanted to make sure I told her what she needed to know. Telling her more than that could keep her up the rest of the night. Not to mention, some things presently outside her awareness could prove dangerous if that knowledge influenced her decisions once we entered Kronto's realm, or the realm of his Hungarian mafia cronies. "Let's move back to the edge of the bed, and we can sit together while I tell you whatever you want."

"You sure this isn't a trick to get me to join you *in* bed?" She laughed softly.

"Well, we'll have to see where your mood is once we have our little talk," I said, and moved to close the door. I checked the lock to make sure it was secure. Meanwhile, she waited for me on the bed, and it took my strongest resolve to not ravish her on the spot.

Immortal Tyranny

"Was that necessary?" She cooed, pointing at the door. "I'm particularly fond of sunsets here, as you know. It does mean you'll have to find someway to make it up to me. On *my* terms."

Her deepening huskiness was driving me nuts... but I needed to stay focused on telling her enough of the truth to count as 'no bullshit'. Not sure why I suddenly worried about uninvited guests showing up. Those familiar with my physical prowess know I'm unafraid of most predators, since it takes a direct hit to my most-vital organs to kill me. Then again, Beatrice's remarkable return to full youth had admittedly heightened my protective instincts. No, she's not a frail-bodied weakling by any stretch. Yet, as mentioned earlier, a mortal wound could kill her—same as it would kill Alistair, Amy, or any other vibrant twenty-something kid.

I worried some of what caused Alistair's recent youthful perspective of invincibility might also occur in this gorgeous young woman who once managed a tough Scottish pub clientele at the end of World War II. Hell, it was the very thing that attracted me when I first laid eyes on Beatrice as a feisty barmaid.

To cloak the extent of my worry, I casually glanced around the two-room cabin, taking in every corner and potential breach while pretending to admire the rustic pine construction. Beatrice had said just a few weeks before that she looked forward to redecorating what had become our retreat from the others. She planned to begin with the stuffed moose head overlooking the mantel.

"It really is dreadful," she said, after my gaze lingered on it for a moment. "But, I would keep everything else largely the way it is. Just add a blend of antiques and a more comfortable bed." She patted the mattress as if afraid a coil might suddenly poke through.

I chuckled at the irony how she and Alistair insisted on the latest comfort designs available back in D.C., before their regeneration blessed them with the resilience of youth.

"What, you don't think I can make it really nice in here?"

She feigned offense, with pouted Emmett Kelly lips.

"I think you'll make it incredibly nice," I said, realizing I was stalling. I took a deep breath and slowly exhaled. "Okay, I will try to give you everything as straight as I can. Do you want me to include our layover in New York tomorrow morning?"

"If you think it's important, then include it," she said, grinning as she noticed my gaze drifted more than once to her nakedness beneath her short gown. "Otherwise, try to stay focused. I'd hate to get dressed... but I'll do whatever it takes to help you come clean."

Such a smartass! She smiled demurely with a sugary tone as she said this last part. Two could play that game.

"As you wish, sweetheart," I said, smiling playfully. But before she could call my bluff I jumped into the meat of it. "The biggest thing Roderick and I will be watching for is Krontos' Hungarian hoodlums seeking to take us out, either in New York or in Germany. He's not going to be pleased we're defying his orders, and he might come after us. Or, he might not."

I paused to make sure she was with me. Her expression had become somber, and she nodded for me to continue.

"I would be lying to you if I said there is no danger in this journey overseas," I confessed, studying her eyes. Stoic, tough, and impossible to read. I could almost feel the steel armor closing around her heart. She was correct in indicating she could handle the picture I was about to paint for her. "Roderick and I will keep our eyes peeled, and you and Alistair will be our first priority—we will protect you both at all costs. Cedric has agreed to look after Amy."

"He's not an immortal... or is he now? If he's not, then what good will he do her?"

"He's still mortal," I said, glancing again around the room. As far as I could tell, no one—namely Krontos—was peeking in on us. Then again, it's not like he would give us a heads-up when he planned to drop by. "But he has over thirty years CIA experience, dealing with some of the deadliest criminals in the world. Add his newfound youth to a skill set like that gives her the best protection possible, outside of an immortal."

She nodded thoughtfully. One less concern to address.

"When we get to Germany—if we get out of New York without a hitch—Roderick and I will likely leave the rest of you at the hotel while we make arrangements about the coin."

"You mean, you want us out of the way while you and Roderick seek to steal it." She eyed me knowingly.

"Yes... that is the plan."

"What about the other two coins? Are you going to try to get them, too?"

Damn. I didn't want to talk about that, since any plan to try and capture anything beyond the Stutthof-Auschwitz coin was secondary. In all likelihood, succeeding in our main objective would be all we accomplished. It would be a mad race back to the states. Eluding Krontos' reach, whether his sorcery or his legion of mercenary crooks, was a tall order with dubious prospects.

"This is crazy... you do know that, right?" she said, revealing her misgivings. "I can't possibly be the only one worried we might not all make it back safely. You feel it, too, do you not?"

Yes, I did. Worried sick about it, truth be told. But what other options were there? At some point, Krontos would come to call with bloody designs—likely I'd lose everyone I cared about, if we sat around waiting on his whims. Traveling as a group entailed more danger, for certain, and yet separating in order to try and shelter the mortals in our six-pack would likely never work. By now, Krontos had made connections to each of us, and we were stronger and more viable as a group, rather than divided into smaller cells.

"You feel it, too... right?" Beatrice persisted.

"Okay, you win," I told her. "We are either sitting ducks or moving targets. Either way is bad. But if we can somehow get to the coin before Krontos does—and believe me, we're worried he might try to do the same thing we're doing—we will have the upper hand."

She shook her head sadly.

"We have a chance, Bea, truly we do." I started to take her in my arms, but she motioned for me to wait.

"I have another question, first, William," she said, and then took my face gently in her hands, forcing my gaze to meet hers. I hate it when she does this. "Have you considered what might happen if you do get the Holocaust Coin and the other two blood coins, and safely add them to your collection?"

"They'll be safe. And the world will be safer—"

"And you'll only lack two coins before you leave us!"

What in the hell?!

"That's not true."

It's what I said. But it felt like a lie as the words left my mouth. And, she knew it—whether in her heart or from my guilt-laden expression.

"It is true, my love," she said. Tears welled in her eyes and her shoulders trembled. "I'm young again, which is wonderful. Wonderful, as long as you are here with me! With Alistair, and Amy, too. I'm even becoming fond of Roderick and Cedric.... But if you're no longer here, I don't believe I can bear it. It was hell the first time you left my life. How much worse will it be the next time?"

"I will never—"

"Shhhh!" She placed her index finger upon my lips to shut me up. "Yes, you will leave, William. Your long, incredible stay on Earth is nearing the end. Can you not see that? Your coins are coming up faster, and faster—Alistair is right about it. And, if you do recover three coins this time, it stands to reason that the last two coins to reach thirty are right around the corner."

She looked as if she had more to say. But the terrible fear of losing me again became too unbearable to hold back any longer. A rain of tears poured forth, followed by terrible wails of grief. As if I had already died, or attained the very thing I had sought for centuries. Reunion with The Almighty. Finally.

It broke my heart to see her like this, and I overcame her resistance, taking her lovingly into my arms. I let her cry until the tears were no more, and then I held her close. She fell asleep before me, and I listened to her shallow breaths become deeper. The night sky lightened, and sometime before the early light of dawn reached Sedona, I joined her.

If only my rest came without dreams I would remember later. Dreams of sorrow... dreams of death.

Chapter Seven

Traveling to New York with Beatrice by my side fulfilled a dream we had talked about since our courtship nearly seventy years ago. She had wanted to spend a day in the heart of New York City. Just one day… and if I hadn't bailed on her and Alistair in Scotland long ago, we might've fulfilled that dream by the late 1950s or early 60s. Definitely would've done so by the time she accompanied our boy to America to attend college.

Although we weren't able to catch the Broadway show Beatrice had envisioned attending since our early days together, she was quite pleased with what we managed to squeeze into one afternoon and evening, on October 27th. Walking through Times Square, Central Park, shopping at the Tiffany flagship store on Fifth Ave, standing atop the Empire

Immortal Tyranny

State Building and Statue of Liberty. The list goes on, and was just as magical for Alistair and Amy, who alone joined us.

Roderick and Cedric had seen the sights around the city hundreds of times—as had I, admittedly. But seeing these points of interest with the woman and son I cherish above all others made the visit incredibly special. As for our two absentees, they spent the day finalizing our itinerary for Germany. Roderick had a panicked air about him, and I almost asked him about it. But things were a little tense between us, after I insisted on spending an extra day in New York to fulfill an overdue promise to Beatrice and Alistair.

"I hope it was worth it, Judas," said Roderick, when we returned to our hotel that evening, the Hyatt-Regency. Some might have expected us to be foolish enough to stay in the Ritz Carlton, to thumb our noses at Krontos Lazarevic, since in all likelihood he was already back in Europe. "Costing us a full day to track down the coin's possessor might come back to bite us in the ass. Michael told me this afternoon that Thomas Wilburn has made contact with the dealer, and will have everything we need concerning this guy once we arrive in Berlin tomorrow evening. But that could've been tonight."

I expected him to wait for a response, but he turned and strode purposely to his room at the end of the hall. Cedric had already turned in, since our flight overseas was at 6:40 a.m.

"See you in the morning, Rod."

"Yep."

"What was that all about?" asked Beatrice, from behind me.

"Nothing, my dear," I assured her. "We will see him and Cedric at breakfast."

But it wasn't 'nothing'. And, I especially hate it when my druid buddy is clairvoyantly spot on with his misgivings.

Despite this encounter's uneasiness, I kept things jovial with Beatrice, Alistair, and Amy. They needed a full night's sleep, and everyone but me was out cold by nine o'clock. I pictured Cedric with a bottle of cognac in his suite, since liquor hadn't been completely sworn off in his new life. Having faced many a day with zero sleep after a night of carousing from his late forties to the time of his transformation in his early sixties, I had no qualms about him burning through the bottle until dawn.

Roderick, on the other hand, worried me. Despite our shared ability to go days without rest, stress had always taken a bigger toll on him than on me. Dark circles had appeared beneath his eyes in the past few days, and now I had added to that stress by delaying our trans-Atlantic journey by nearly sixteen hours from an earlier available flight.

Did I worry about forgiveness if my lollygagging turned out to be costly? Not after nineteen hundred years of transgressions, one to another. But, certainly it could make things uncomfortable while I waited for his irritation to wane.

That's what I expected. Here's what I didn't expect.

"There's been a 'development'," he told me the next morning.

We had already checked in our luggage and made it through security at LaGuardia Airport. At the moment, I sat between Alistair and Cedric, as Beatrice and Amy were engaged in girl talk to where my son finally had enough and took a rare opportunity to hobnob with his old man.

"Meaning what?" I asked.

Beneath his amber-tinted sunglasses, I could see the cyclone of gold specs immersed in Roderick's glowing blue irises. In other words, I had just pissed him off with my flippant response. To his credit, he caught himself in time to not berate me for my reckless behavior in front of everyone else. He released an exasperated sigh.

"Our contact, Thomas Wilburn?"

"Yeah, what about him."

"He's disappeared—*that's* what about him!"

"What in the hell?!"

"My thoughts exactly, William," he said. His voice momentarily went into surround sound as he trembled from anger. "Michael says the dealer holding the coin is also missing. He has already called in the best teams to search for Thomas and our dealer.... If you hadn't been such a selfish ass and stayed focused on our business, we might've gotten there quickly enough to save Thomas, and likely retrieved your coin!"

He turned away, shaking his head as he prepared to sit down in the row of seats across the way. Largely deserted at this hour, our gals and a young blonde woman with her two toddlers playing at her feet were the only other occupants.

"You don't know that," I said, softly. Roderick hesitated before taking a seat. But he didn't turn to face me... yet. "Krontos has outsmarted us at nearly every turn. You know this, my brother. Who's to say he wasn't prepared to make his move at any time? Perhaps, he's been waiting on us to make our move first."

No response, and I confirmed the bristling from Alistair and Cedric was more directed at me than at Roderick. Their matching uncomfortable expressions told me as much. Apparently, they hoped I would take my tongue-lashing from Roderick and drop the issue. At least the young mom cast me an empathetic glance. But, Beatrice's cautionary nod served as the strongest reminder this should be a private spat. Meanwhile, Roderick's response was a mere huff. He sat down and gazed past me to the large terminal window, as if I was no longer present.

Too bad he and Krontos weren't on better terms, as our adversary might be all too willing to grant that wish.

"Very funny," Roderick deadpanned, drawing looks from our companions, who then turned their attention to me.

"Sorry. Truly, Roderick, I am."

I frowned, considering he might be right in what I had unwittingly rendered by wanting to spend a meaningful New York moment with my wife and kid. Before anyone suggests I could've waited until our mission was finished, life doesn't always play out that neatly. Those who have dealt with the untimely loss of a loved one know exactly what I'm talking about. Tomorrow is promised to no one.

"So, are we still going to fly to Germany, or should we see if we can cancel our tickets and get a refund?" Amy asked, when her quiet conversation with Beatrice reached its end.

"Germany's a pretty country, man," said Cedric, putting his laptop back inside its case. He eyed us all, wearing the smirk Roderick and I have long loathed. "But this time of year? Man, it's starting to get frigging cold out there. So, I'm in agreement with Amy. If we aren't one hundred percent sure about this, then let's cancel this cluster-fuck before things get worse."

And so it went for the next twenty minutes, until eight minutes remained before our flight began boarding. I believe all of us waited for Roderick to stick a permanent dagger into our trip, since his brooding deflated the group's waning enthusiasm. I might've gone with the flow, especially when considering Beatrice's lament from the night before. Venture overseas, and though increasingly unlikely, I might return home to the States with three more silver shekels, lacking just two more to find. Or, return now to Sedona, and let the winds of fate take Krontos and his evil designs where they may. Long-term survival would be dicey, but having five coins missing from my collection could ensure a blissful life with my family that lasted decades, if not centuries.

"We must go to Germany," I announced, picking up my laptop and preparing to head to the boarding area once the ticket counter attendant made her first call for the first class passengers to prepare boarding the airplane. "Despite all the bullshit going on, it is where we're supposed to be. Whatever comes next will be revealed when we get there."

The conviction in my voice surprised everyone. It wasn't what I expected—not from any of us, and definitely not from me. But, as I began to visualize our return to the ranch, a peculiar sensation suddenly flowed through my entire being. With it came the conviction I needed to find Krontos and stop him from whatever he was planning to do next—even if it meant everyone else remained in America.

"Are you sure?" Roderick stood and removed his sunglasses to study me, for the moment unconcerned someone might glimpse his preternatural eyes.

"Yes, I am," I assured him, glancing at Beatrice, who couldn't hide her disappointment. Her smile till now had been a façade, being a good sport on behalf of everyone else. But the talk of retreating to Sedona had given her hope we would abort the trip overseas. I shot her a loving look before returning my gaze to Roderick. "I feel the weight of The Almighty's hand upon my soul. There will be no peace until we resolve our feud with Krontos. The situation goes beyond our little group. We must find a way to stop him, or live to regret what he intends to bring upon every nation that stands in his way."

Roderick nodded and smiled, surely surprised and pleased by my apparent change of mind. Cedric smiled, too, as if this was the course of action he preferred all along—despite his most recent comments. But for my beloved wife, kid, and soon to be daughter-in-law, there was only sadness.

* * * * *

"I hope you know what in the hell you're doing this time, Pops."

Alistair sipped on the nine-hour flight's first gin and tonic, while looking out over the Atlantic from his window seat. He and I sat together in the first class section of the Delta jumbo-jet to Berlin. Comfortably sandwiched between Roderick and Cedric in front of us, and Beatrice and Amy behind, all of us intended to share each other's company throughout the flight. However, my recent unpopularity with my immortal buddy and beloved wife would certainly impact how long poor Alistair had to tolerate his old man's presence.

Of course, I'm joking... well, sort of.

"Me, too, Ali." I nursed my preferred scotch on the rocks. It seemed far too early in the day for liquor, but I hated to see my son drink alone. Too many bad memories of what things were like for him when I re-entered his life, shortly after he began work on his master's degree in South Carolina. "But you and Roderick have always admonished me to not ignore the Lord's bidding."

"And you're sure that's what it is this time?" He eyed me seriously. "Are you sure you're not in a hurry to secure three coins at once, instead of just one?"

"You sound like your mother," I teased quietly, though realizing Beatrice's sonic ears—or even Amy's—might land me in deeper purgatory. "As I assured her, I'm in no hurry to leave any of you here. I know you and I haven't spent as much time together as we used to. I miss that, Ali, more than you know. But, life has its ebbs and flows, and I have no doubt you and I will be spending lots of quality time together again before you know it. Your mother and I look forward to more double dates like the one we did last month, when the four of us flew to San Francisco for a weekend. And, down the road, after you and Amy are married and have had time to establish your own roots—"

"Pops, as long as villains like Krontos Lazarevic and Viktor Kaslow exist, hoping for anything beyond exchanging our vows together is foolish," he said, shutting down the fatherly talk before it got rolling. "Not to be harsh—I know you mean well. But, we are at war. Or, more accurately, we are refugees fleeing a madman who is completely unpredictable. We might find him, or his mafia, waiting for us at Schönefeld Airport, or in the lobby at the Esplanade Hotel in Berlin."

"And to think that sort of thing used to excite you," I mused, trying not to chuckle. "Of course, having the women we cherish along for the ride raises the stakes significantly. Hard to embrace the adventure when that's the case, I know."

"Hey, I heard that," chimed in Amy from behind us. "I'd say your cherished women have held up pretty damned well in the past."

"Yes, you have," I replied, while sharing the pain in Alistair's grimace. He would be lost without her, as I would without Beatrice. It brought to mind how close the gals came to meeting their end at the hands of Dracul, less than five months earlier. And, yet, neither one had ever mentioned the experience, because it was wiped clean from their reality.

Roderick and I alone still held the experience of me nearly losing Beatrice, Amy, and Alistair in Dracul's castle of horrors. Not to mention our horrified surprise to later learn it was Krontos pulling the dimensional shifts that altered the event imprint upon our particular earth plane. Only a master of metaphysics could fully appreciate experiencing one very real set of events being overridden permanently by a totally different outcome than originally perceived.

"And, unlike last time, when we flew overseas to find you, maybe we can actually participate," Amy added.

Her words seemed to drain the color from Alistair's face. Despite his increasing carelessness as he regained his youth, he still knew better than to tempt fate. He didn't need to share Roderick's and my near brush with death in Montenegro to know what Krontos was capable of. And, yet, he didn't dare sound weak in front of his fiancée.

"Only if absolutely necessary, babe," he said, raising himself to gaze at her over his seat. He added a bright, confident smile. "I'm all for a little adventure in hunting for a coin or two, but I do think we'd be at a distinct disadvantage in a gun battle with the mafia dudes Roderick and Cedric described."

"Only if they're packing the latest assault rifles," said Cedric from in front of us. "Otherwise it might be a fair fight." He chuckled, and I do believe Alistair could've strangled him for stoking the fire.

"The biggest thing is to be precise with our decisions and movements in response to what we find in Berlin," said Roderick, for the moment not turning around to look at us. Thankfully, he had the foresight to purchase the other seats in our curtained-off section ahead of time. Still, voices carry—especially my druid buddy's voice when he gets on a roll. "And, since none of us fully understands how Krontos is able to eavesdrop from anywhere, and affect changes to environment, interactions, time, etc., I think it would be best if we kept things loose and unfocused on why we've made this trip. Perhaps a new joke or two that we've recently heard in Sedona, or we can settle for one of William's or Cedric's colorful spy stories to start us off. Just anything that has nothing to do with why we're here."

The chuckles and sidebar conversation between Beatrice and Amy abruptly stopped. Talk about a wet blanket on a dying fire. Well played, Roderick.

Immortal Tyranny

When the silence turned awkward, roughly a minute after his admonishment, Alistair snickered to himself.

"What's so funny?" I asked.

"What if all this precaution stuff is for naught?" he said thoughtfully. "What if Krontos has already played his first move in this latest cat and mouse routine, and we are already unwitting lab mice working through the maze he's created?"

Indeed. It's not like Roderick or I hadn't considered this possibility before then. But hearing it from Alistair's lips made it sound much more chilling. From that moment until we landed in Berlin, it was all I could think about. It took nearly every trick I could muster to maintain a casual and merry persona, telling my botched espionage tales with humor, gusto, and Cedric's colorful asides. All the while, I wondered and worried how cruel and extensive Krontos' elaborate trap for us could be.

Chapter Eight

It was just after nine o'clock that night when we landed in Berlin, and most of us were affected by jetlag. Well, those of us not named Roderick or myself were affected. Frankly, I was a bit surprised at the severity, since Alistair, Amy, and Beatrice had flown a further distance in June, when they followed Alistair's whim to pursue Roderick and me in Rome and then they pressed on to Budva.

As for Cedric, after the many hundreds of thousands of frequent flyer miles he had accumulated during his time with the CIA, I was surprised by his disorientation, too. Tampara and the Yitari people Cedric lived with in Bolivia had transformed his body into one suited for their realm. I guess that meant he was now a novice air traveler in our world, and would have to learn the ropes all over again. Even so, I expected him to be ready for our breakfast meeting by Skype with Michael.

The good news, as far as Roderick and I could tell, was our reality seemed to be intact. It felt natural to our deepest instincts and nothing seemed off thus far, which was a relief. In fact, neither of us sensed Krontos' presence in any fashion—including the absence of his thugs.

"It might just be the three of us at breakfast, I believe," I told Roderick, after we had checked into our rooms at the Grand Hotel Esplanade. Although, I heard a television on in Alistair and Amy's room, Beatrice was fast asleep by the time I met Roderick by the vending machines near our fifth floor accommodations. "I'll stop by Cedric's room on the way to your room. Shall we do room service?"

"It may be best, since Michael is expecting us to start at seven, and it might take a moment to get everything set up," he said. "Hopefully, he will surprise us with good news about Thomas and Franz Riefenstahl."

"Who is Franz Rifenstahl?"

"That's the dealer… Michael sent a text earlier with what they had learned about him," Roderick explained, after cautiously scanning the hallway. We were definitely alone. "Look, we can go over this in my room tonight, or when you stop by in the morning."

As tempting as it was to get the details right then, often these updates can turn out much longer than expected. Especially in a situation like this, where my own curiosity about what happened to Agent Wilburn and the German guy named Riefenstahl was heightened. Then there was also the story behind the obvious protocol breach of enlisting CIA personnel for this mission—highly inappropriate. My assumption was that it came as an owed favor to Roderick, and at worst, would be treated as a harmless misappropriation if

Thomas made it out of this alive. Roderick's expression told me this wasn't likely, and would have additional unpleasant news to share with Cedric and me at daybreak.

"It can wait until morning," I said, grasping his shoulder as I held him in my gaze. "I don't often say it, Rod, but I really appreciate you. Thank you for sticking with me and keeping me on point."

"Are you sure?" he said, smiling impishly. "The dynamic of pursuing your coins is changing. Or, rather, it *has* changed."

He didn't have to spell it out, as it was the exact same thing I had been telling myself since Alistair, and later, Beatrice, got younger. My passion for ending my long stay on this earth was waning. Instead, I was becoming more and more like the other immortals we've known for so many centuries. None of them are in a hurry to die. Just me, and now it was no longer the case.

"I'm sure."

I watched him move down the hall to his room. Just like in our Sedona ranch home, he preferred his distance. But at least we parted ways that night wearing smiles. Maybe, it could be the thing to bridge the gap between us that had steadily widened for far too long.

* * * * *

Beatrice slept harder than she had in months—her need for rest likely impacted by her stress-laden misgivings from the past few days. After leaving her a note reminding her I would be in Roderick's suite, should she need me, I set the Do Not Disturb sign outside our door and stepped over to Cedric's room across the way, quietly moving past Alistair and Amy's room. There was no answer when I knocked, and for a moment I worried something had happened to him while I slept.

"Please tell me Cedric is here," I told Roderick, as he opened his door to let me in. "Everyone else is sleeping."

"Gotta admit I'm touched, Willie Boy," said Cedric, calling from beyond the partition separating the living area from the bedroom. "I don't think I've ever heard you sound this worried about my welfare!"

He peered around the corner, smiling wryly with a steaming cup of coffee in hand.

"Good to see another vice has returned," I teased, offering a knowing smirk to Roderick as I stepped inside. "When did you resume the caffeine?"

"This morning. Right after Roderick told me the news," said Cedric, motioning for me to come over to the dinette, where an array of pastries surrounded two tall silver pots, one for coffee and the other tea. "I'm damned close to opening the floodgates to all my vices, William. You heard the latest shit yet? If you haven't, you might want to hit Roderick up for a highball or two to go with breakfast." He pointed to the scotch bottles sitting atop the mini-fridge.

"I hope it doesn't come to that," I said, feeling my smile fade. The look on Roderick's face confirmed the revelation wasn't going to be pleasant.

"Michael will be joining us on video in about fifteen minutes," said Roderick, moving over to the dinette to pour himself a cup of coffee. He motioned to see if I wanted one, and I waved him off for the moment. "I wish I had good news to report."

He moved to his laptop sitting open on a coffee table, and turned it toward me.

"The Berlin police fished out two bodies from the River Spree last night," said Roderick, playing a German news broadcast from the night before, showing emergency vehicles gathered close to a river's edge. "Michael sent his latest update at four o'clock this morning, confirming the bodies are Agent Wilburn and Mr. Riefenstahl. The official autopsy reports will take a few days, but Michael said both bodies appear to have multiple gunshot wounds."

"Execution at the hands of Krontos' cronies?"

"Likely. But until the bodies are processed, we won't know for sure," Roderick advised, sitting down on the couch. Cedric joined him and the pair cleared a spot for me to sit front and center to the laptop. It appeared I'd be the featured attraction for Skype time with Michael. Oh joy. "The internet links to the auction site have been disabled. We can only assume the coin is now in the perpetrators' possession, and I expect they will be purging all on-line evidence of the coin's existence."

"So, Krontos has it in his possession, or will soon," I said, stating the obvious conclusion to no one in particular. "Should we also assume he will somehow find a way to remove the awareness of the coin from the world's consciousness? Or, do you think he will only seek to eliminate it from our awareness?"

"What... and perhaps alter the entire series of events that led us here?" Roderick frowned as he pulled the laptop toward him, typing in new commands.

"Wait... wait a goddamned minute!" Cedric reached over me to prevent Roderick from typing. "You two need to speak straight, instead of this 'altered world' bullshit. There's no way some dude—immortal or not—can do things not even God can!"

"You mean the altered reality we encountered in Bolivia, and which once formed the only protection for the Yitari's long, peaceful existence, is a bunch of bullshit, too?" countered Roderick, just as irritated. "How did you ever make it back home from the dimensional plane you spent six months residing in? Hmmmm? You didn't just hop on a Greyhound bus to the States from the shores of Lake Titicaca, did you? Not to mention, how do you explain the time passage of several years in the six months spent away from our plane that you told us about in June? You, better than anyone, should understand the rules governing time and events are not the same when going from one dimension to another!"

The pair eyed each other angrily, but said nothing more. I took the opportunity to see if I could present an explanation that made sense to Cedric. Otherwise, the rest of our breakfast meeting could remain volatile, and therefore unproductive.

"I know you think all the new age metaphysical stuff out there is pure nonsense, Cedric," I said, turning to face him. "And for the most part, you are totally correct. But, some metaphysical principles are rooted in and supported by traditional science. Even Einstein bought into some of it, as mentioned before. But let me begin explaining things to you like this: Everyone has free will to make countless choices in life, correct?"

He nodded curtly, the anger hovering near the surface.

"Suppose every one of those choices you could've made in our reality still exists elsewhere, with real outcomes on some other plane, or planes, of existence. For example, you told me once you dreamt of being a sculptor when you graduated from college, and you also regretted not pursuing your baseball dream with the Los Angeles Dodgers when they recruited you out of high school—things you thought were impractical. Instead, you chose what seemed wiser and financially sustainable. And, that choice eventually led to one hell of a career with the CIA. But... what if those other choices you thought hard about and didn't act upon became reality somewhere else?"

"That really sounds like bullshit, William" he said, snickering. "If that's the best you can do, all your efforts to change my mind won't do jack!"

"Okay… I'll give you that, my friend," I said, glancing at Roderick. "But humor us anyway, since what if the facts in this case end up pointing to our bizarre premise being the truth?"

Cedric snickered again, but indicated he would politely listen to the rest of what came pouring out of my mouth. Roderick bristled beside me.

"From what we can tell, Krontos has not only figured out how to travel within other dimensions, such as the ones you witnessed in Bolivia. He has also learned how to cultivate the alternative realities of other people, and superimpose snippets into their lives on this earth plane," I said, ignoring the growing mirth in Cedric's eyes. "If such a thing was possible, can you at least picture what would happen to those posing the biggest threat to his designs? And, how would they know he had altered their lives by grafting in either negative or positive events on a whim?"

"Sounds like surgery… of the bullshit variety," he replied. But, at least he was hearing me—even if he couldn't wrap his mind around it all.

"Precisely," said Roderick, his tone extending forgiveness for their recent spat. "It is just like surgery. And it doesn't have to be full-scale alternate lifetimes Krontos taps into for him to accomplish his goals. He can take a weekend, or a day. Hell, we've seen him take an hour or two from a person's earthly reality and replace it with a completely different sequence of events lifted from one of their alternative paths that never came to fruition in our world."

I didn't feel the need to add anything else. Neither did Roderick. The ball was in Cedric's court, and all we could do was hope he would eventually become open to this way of thinking. At some point, his survival would likely depend on it.

Meanwhile, it was time to meet with Michael Lavoie.

Seeing my former CIA boss for the first time in nearly two and a half years was good, at least for the most part. Awkward at first, since it took a moment to get used to the physical changes as viewed through the slightly distorted transmission received by Roderick's Macbook. Father time was finally winning the war with Michael's vanity. His face was fuller, with unflattering definition to his surgically altered jowls, and I briefly detected a slight paunch around his waistline. Not that I'd ever judge anyone for these imperfections, as they are part of the natural aging process. But, since Michael had liked to poke fun at others for having these flaws, I couldn't suppress a slight grin.

"So, what will you boys be doing now?" asked Michael, after our debriefing ended.

"Well, we had planned to be here through November first, and our flight back to the States isn't until the afternoon of the second," said Roderick. "Maybe we will have a look around."

Sounded fine to me. Maybe we could revisit some of the places I had last seen in the spring of 1945, shortly after Germany's surrender. Maybe I could figure out something romantic to help ease my wife's trepidation in coming here. Lord knows there would be sightseeing that Alistair and Amy would be up for.

"I strongly suggest you not do that," advised Michael. "We may not understand Krontos on your level, but we have seen the murderous rampages his thugs participate in. Who's to say you're not on a hit list right now? I would like for you all to come back to Washington, and to do it tonight. Don't delay."

"Mike, you're sounding like a boss—*our* boss," said Cedric. He glanced at Roderick and me before going on. "But none of us work for you anymore. You, my friend, are strictly an advisor at this point. And, though we'll take your advisement under consideration, you'll likely have to find some other way to cover your ass for Thomas's death."

I expected Michael to offer a harsh rebuke. I had been privy to a few of those down through the years. But, he merely nodded, before confirming if that was also Roderick's and my position.

"We will make it without your watchdogs, Michael," said Roderick, to which I agreed. "We understand that if we get in over our heads, we'll have to work things out on our own. There will be no safety net from you or anyone else back in Washington this time."

I shot Roderick a look, since I assumed this had been the way things were since I rebuffed the agency's efforts to get me to come back, six months before our Bolivia trip last year. He mouthed an assurance he would explain things at a later time, and we wrapped up our video meeting with Michael.

"So, what are we going to do?" I asked Roderick. "Or, more accurately, what can I tell Beatrice and Alistair?"

"We can go home, if you insist," he said. "Or, we could see some sights for a few days, making sure we all wear bullet proof vests."

"Or, we can go find this son of a bitch," said Cedric. "If it were up to me, I'd want to be hunting Krontos, instead of the other way around."

He had a point. They both did.

"Maybe we can see a few sights while we pursue Krontos," I said, at first not sure why I suggested such a thing. But as I thought about it, it started to make sense. Crazy sense. "Until we know for sure he has the coin, I think we should try to get closer to him. Closer, but not too close."

"Now, what in the hell are you talking about?" Cedric released an exasperated sigh.

"Actually, it might be something that works well," said Roderick, smiling at me. He must've liked the puzzle pieces coming together in my head. "Even though it's likely Krontos already has the coin, it's foolish to assume this outcome without a little research. Maybe a visit to the very places that made this coin famous could hone William's senses to be drawn to where it is."

"Stutthof and Auschwitz?" I whispered, seeing the connection Roderick had picked up on.

"We've got almost four days before our scheduled flight, which saves me the hassle of canceling and rebooking," he said, his smile widening. "We just need to secure some weaponry… just in case."

He picked up his phone, and soon scanned his contacts.

"I thought we told Mike to take a frigging hike?" Cedric eyed him suspiciously.

"We did," said Roderick. "But the CIA isn't the only game in town."

And, so, we prepared to embark on the next leg of our journey. An excursion Roderick and Cedric seemed pleased about, with reactions I never would have pictured just two days earlier. Staying in Europe would be a tougher sell to Beatrice… not sure about my boy and his gal.

My biggest concern at the moment was the presence of a nagging doubt refusing to go away. A counsel cautioning me to reflect on what I had lectured Cedric about earlier. Was the inspiration spawning our latest plans an earthly perception? Or did it come from somewhere else?

I sent an urgent prayer heavenward, that it wasn't Krontos feeding me a path from one of my alternative existences.

Chapter Nine

"Why in the hell did we even bother coming up here if there is no coin to find? Maybe we should return to Roderick's fortress in America. Surely, Krontos has moved on by now."

Alistair's complaint carried validity to a point, and only because Roderick, Cedric, and I decided not to tell him the full reason as to why we were visiting Stutthof. All we revealed to him and Amy was the same advisement I gave Beatrice when I returned to our room: The auction was off, the coin was missing, and our CIA contact was dead.

Plenty to digest, considering she had awakened only thirty minutes earlier.

Unlike Alistair, she at least waited for the subplots to be filled in before reacting to my announcement of traveling to Poland. Once I told her we wanted to see if anything, psychic or otherwise, came to Roderick or me when visiting the Nazi death camps involved with the coin, she offered only a slight protest. Her biggest qualm was making sure we didn't linger in Europe any longer than our original plans. I could tell she was intrigued by the prospects of visiting memorials from World War II. Although, dealing with cooler weather than Germany's balmy October temperatures meant she would need a warmer coat prior to making the trek to Northern Poland.

"If it turns out we get nothing, in terms of impressions or the tingling that can sometimes reach my left arm from half the world away, then we'll head back to Berlin tomorrow night and see if we can reschedule our flight back to the States a day early," I replied to Alistair, looking toward Stutthof's main entrance as Cedric parked our rental. "You really need to lighten up on the stress, Ali. Seriously, son."

I heard his familiar 'humpf' from the backseat he shared with Amy, thinking it sounded more endearing when he was a soon to be retired college professor. Beatrice and I occupied the middle bench of the minivan, and Roderick kept Cedric company in the front. My wife rolled her eyes, and at first I thought she was ready to chide me. But then she cut a scornful glance at our boy.

"Krontos breached the fortress easily the first time," added Roderick, adjusting his coat and fedora. Cedric unlocked the doors and we gathered our cameras and notepads. Roderick made the brilliant suggestion for us all to take pictures and notes—to not just rely on the paranormally gifted in our midst. "You might be right that he won't return there. However, since he has invaded our lives effortlessly on a whim, wouldn't it be nice if we had a few less questions about the coin's whereabouts the next time he comes to call?"

"Only if you find the damned thing before we return home on Monday," replied Alistair. "Otherwise, all you're doing is wasting precious time."

Everyone exited the van, with Roderick pausing to make sure the guns he and Cedric procured while I entertained my family at their breakfast meal in the hotel's main dining room were still camouflaged by a blanket in the very back. Unless someone with prior knowledge alerted the authorities, I didn't expect any police interference. Roderick acted as if he wasn't so sure, carefully scanning the area around us. The parking area was packed with tourists, likely hoping to beat the wintry weather reportedly on the way by the weekend.

"Remember what we discussed on the way here," Roderick said. "William needs to be the first one inside the camp exhibit, followed by me. Then Beatrice, Ali, and Amy. Cedric will pull up the rear, keeping an eye out just in case."

I gave my wife a loving kiss and moved ahead of everyone else. Roderick adjusted his sunglasses as he kept pace behind me. I had thought there wouldn't be a need for us to be so organized until inside the encampment, but a powerful feeling of déjà vu swept over me as we made our way to the main entrance. Yes, the place had an outdoor museum feel to it, but for the most part it felt as it did when I visited the grounds in late spring, 1945.

"This place is swarming with energy," said Roderick, reverently, behind me.

I had instinctively picked up my pace, and he stayed with me stride for stride. I could hear the others murmuring further behind us about 'what's the big hurry?' I couldn't fight the urge to quickly get beyond the memorial entrance, as if the barracks, towers, and barbwire fences called to me, like long lost friends.

"It's a vortex from hell," I told him, briefly glancing over a shoulder. "Maybe we shouldn't have done this."

"Just be glad you are only feeling the energy pull. Would you rather see and hear the imprints assaulting my mind?"

Very good point. The oppressive sadness that had forever imprinted itself upon this hallowed ground might well overwhelm me before our afternoon visit concluded. However, it was nothing compared to the visual images of unspeakable suffering and cruelty being presented to Roderick's mind in vibrant images. Images in living color, along with the scents and auditory imprints from those events. Olfactory assaults of blood, sweat, human waste, and the terrible stench of burning flesh from the four crematoriums on the property—all serenaded by the screams of agony and cries for mercy from a multitude of victims derided by zealous insults and rebukes from a host of inhuman SS guards.

"Sorry, Rod. We can abort this idea," I told him, as my heart was overwhelmed with compassion for him and the tens of thousands who suffered so horribly, and lost their lives in this place. "I doubt I'll pick up anything about the coin with such a barrage going on."

"We need to try anyway." His voice cracked, and I stopped to let him catch up. He wiped his fingers beneath his glasses that had fogged up. "Keep moving Judas. Like you, I haven't been here in decades... but I feel compelled to do this. If you are reluctant to do it for your coin, then please do it for me."

I nodded and resumed my pace, ignoring Alistair's pleas for me to wait up. Other tourists around us gave Roderick and I strange looks as we hurried to the entrance. Although they had no clue as to why we were in a rush, their somber expressions confirmed they felt the oppressiveness.

"Are you going to be all right, Roderick?" asked Amy, once we began our official tour of the premises. Her eyes were tearing as she studied him. To his credit, he kept himself emotionally together to nod in response. "Are you sure?"

"It's probably best to let him work through this, my dear," I told her gently. "On the way to Krakow, we can discuss what he's picked up on." I offered a compassionate smile that defied the dread threatening to overwhelm me. It wouldn't be long before both Roderick and I would be rendered mute.

The deepening coldness crept into my bones—and surely it sought to invade everyone else. The sound of coats and hoods zipped tightly resounded around us, surely fed by siphoned energy feeding hundreds of souls that never moved on. Not completely unlike my long sentence to roam the earth, those who died in bitter sorrow found it difficult to leave. My eyes began to mist, and I braced my heart for the emotional onslaught about to come.

Beatrice came up to me, wrapping her arms around my waist. Her warmth was most welcome, and the love radiating from her spirit to mine warmed me to the core. But a look from Roderick reminded me of our purpose here. I needed to move to the front of our little group and lead the way.

"I love you."

Her words touched me deeper than her embrace, and I tried to respond in kind. But my voice was just as lost as Roderick's. I nodded and turned away, hoping she never forgot how deeply I cherished her and our incorrigible son.

"Follow me," I whispered.

There were professionally guided tours going on around us. Of course, we didn't participate, instead following the energy flow of the death camp now largely covered in grass and concrete. I had no doubt Roderick would glean important images and messages from imprinted events dating from the

Immortal Tyranny

internment camp's change to a labor education camp in late 1941, until the Allies' liberation in May, 1945. But I worried I wouldn't pick up anything dealing with my legendary coin.

But I was wrong.

Though I didn't actually find anything tangible, I glimpsed a bluish glow inside one barrack, and again, near where a barrack building had once stood, not far from a guard tower and conveniently close to a gas chamber built when the Final Solution included the Jews housed at Stutthof.

"You see it, don't you?" said Roderick from behind me. He sounded calmer than earlier—a sure sign he had managed to get the psychic assault under control. "If only you could see the joy and hope that existed in this barrack. It was one the Nazis loathed the most.... I see their fear and hatred of the building. They learned to avoid it, which was bad for the camp's other inmates.... They took out their fear on the others."

I turned to see his grimacing expression. I wanted to stop him, especially when he announced some of the bloodier atrocities that took place in the barrack still standing next to where the unusual one he alluded to once stood. Beatrice and Amy grimaced worse than him, and even Alistair and Cedric looked like they wished Roderick would shut the hell up about it all. But, he was now a channel for the horrific memories stored here, and the unfortunate commentary from spirits all too eager to share what they endured more than seventy years ago.

"I see the glow," I confessed. "But, it's just a phantom. Obviously, the coin is long since removed from this place. Its essence remains, but is weak."

"The hope of redemption and demonstration of power gave hope to hundreds," said Roderick. "And they're telling me the coin brought death to a few of the guards.... Yes, it did. After the third 'heart attack', the other SS men became superstitious.

Conditions remained bad here, but the inmates were no longer called out in the bitter cold."

Roderick's serious expression suddenly morphed into a giddy smile.

"What's up, man?" asked Cedric, from the rear. Watchful eyes and his hand secured to a Beretta inside his coat pocket, he brought his gaze back to meet Roderick's when he didn't respond right away. "Well?"

"The miracles inside the barrack... they *really* happened!" Roderick enthused. "Bread and fish... I see it appear in between the bunks, and the men and women covering the children's mouths to keep them from crying out in surprise. The coin brought warmth and peace, too. Incredible, since none of your other coins have been like this, William. Correct?"

"As far as I've known they have always brought sorrow and suffering. Nothing more," I said.

Roderick motioned for me to move out further from the barrack no longer there. I approached the barbed wire fence, but felt nothing. Same for the crematorium next to the gas chamber. He was shaking his head as I returned to where he and everyone else stood, near the markers for the barrack's eroded foundation stones.

"Such joy for a moment, and hope that lasted weeks, months... until resentment slipped in here," continued Roderick. His smile faded. "They could've gone many more months, perhaps even years. If not for a jealous young woman and her father... they told the guards about the coin."

"So, the coin was cursed after all," noted Alistair. "What else do you pick up?"

"The Nazis here could never find it, this mystical coin," said Roderick, staggering a moment as he moved into the middle of where the building had stood long ago. "The girl and

Immortal Tyranny

old man were beaten to death, and once that happened, something changed. The coin no longer produced any supernatural effect. It's as if betrayal sucked the life out of it."

"The guards could tell something had changed, I'd be willing to bet," said Alistair. For the moment, his cynical side appeared subdued. Like the rest of us, tears welled in his eyes. Without a better explanation, it seemed we were all somehow tapped into the same energy stream feeding Roderick's vision and my oppression. "What happened after that? Can you tell?"

Hard to say, but the look on Roderick's face told me what happened next was worse than anything he had touched on earlier. This time, he refused to comment on it, stating only that the coin and its owners were removed from the camp—likely related to the earlier accusations. The Nazis were steeped into the occult like no other nation in modern history, and it wouldn't be farfetched to say Stutthof's commandant shipped the burdensome owners of a relic—one that could vanish and reappear in the camp, and definitely hostile to Nazi handlers—someplace else.

To Auschwitz.

Chapter Ten

We didn't arrive in Krakow until almost midnight that evening. Mortals and immortals alike were emotionally drained after our Stutthof visit. Not to mention, the long drive from Germany to Stutthof had made for a very long day. Despite only visiting the camp museum for half an hour, it was almost four o'clock when we arrived. Afterward, Cedric's lead foot couldn't overcome the stops for food and gas as we barreled south toward Auschwitz. Visiting our second camp first thing on the morning of the 30th seemed increasingly unlikely.

After settling for modest accommodations at a small inn just outside the city, we reached a compromise on when to get going in the morning. We agreed to all meet for breakfast at the inn's restaurant at 8:30 a.m. Beatrice and I hardly spoke due to how exhausted she was. She climbed into bed and by the time I joined her, she was fast asleep. A good thing, since I needed a restful night's sleep, as well.

The snowstorm we hoped to avoid reached Krakow overnight, and we hurried through flurries to get the minivan loaded up with our belongings after breakfast. We would arrive at Auschwitz within the hour, around ten-thirty, provided the weather didn't get much worse.

"I spoke to Benevento early this morning," Roderick announced, once everyone was settled and we began our trek.

"Oh? Did he give you any new information on Krontos and my coin?" I asked.

Our seating arrangements were slightly different from yesterday, as Beatrice and Amy elected to sit together. That left Alistair and me to a potential 'father-son chat, part two' episode. We let the ladies occupy the middle seat, leaving us in the very back of the vehicle. Not the most conducive arrangement for Roderick's update, since it left him no choice but to allow his preternatural voice to fill the van.

"Nothing new," said Roderick, turning around in the passenger seat to face me, while Cedric pulled onto the main highway heading west from Krakow. "However, when I told him we had visited Stutthof yesterday afternoon, and were set to visit Auschwitz this morning, he pointed out a few things connected to the coin, Krontos, and these two terrible centers of death."

I nodded for him to go on. He had everyone's attention, including Cedric's.

"Although none of us can prove Krontos has the coin in his possession—or in his thugs' possession—Benevento is certain Krontos is up to his neck in this shit. In fact, Krontos is up to his neck in everything we're dealing with—including the terrible tragedy that created the environment enabling the Stutthof-Auschwitz coin to play such a unique role in 1944."

"The Holocaust?" Alistair sought to confirm.

"Yes, the Holocaust," said Roderick. "The Vatican has long known that Krontos actively supported the Nazis in many of their endeavors. Everything from the Final Solution's strategic implementations to providing the Third Reich's scientists with futuristic technology to ensure they conquered the world."

"The same stuff you and I discussed the other night. Correct?" I preferred not to rehash everything in front of everyone else, and hoped we could keep things to the latest information from Benevento. "I don't suppose the Vatican is ready to delve out more details about Krontos using his dimensional travel prowess to jump to the 1980s and pilfer the blueprints for the stealth bomber and other nifty toys and deliver them to the Nazis?"

"What?! Run that by me again, Pops!"

Alistair's surprise was echoed by the gals and Cedric, prompting a hostile glare directed at me from my druid buddy.

"If this is true, it seems the Germans would have won the war," said Alistair, his tone irritated. Obviously, he considered this as another instance of immortal bullshit—nearly impossible to prove or disprove. "But they didn't win."

"They ran out of time to implement the plans on the stealth," said Roderick, wearing a smug smile. It likely would have been a more somber look had my boy not responded like an ass. "There were other technological advances in the works as well, and yes, the Germans would have won the conflict in Europe and likely conquered the rest of the world by 1950. But according to a secret diary in the Vatican's possession, a diary attributed to Heinrich Himmler, the Nazis' betrayal of Krontos is what brought them down."

I didn't expect to hear a revelation like this. Neither did anyone else, after a quick scan of everyone's expressions. Time for me to get the details I needed to fully understand the scope of this bombshell.

"So, Krontos is named in the journal you're talking about?" I asked, for the moment ignoring the scrutinizing looks from Alistair, Amy, and Beatrice. "I'm surprised anything clandestine in some circles would be openly discussed elsewhere—especially in a Nazi's personal memoir."

"He's not specifically named," said Roderick, turning in his seat to face me fully. "Here's what Benevento told me is written by Himmler. 'We trusted the Hungarian madman, especially the Fuhrer. Most of us—meaning Hitler's staff—followed blindly, and enthusiastically endorsed the madman's insistence on ancient occult symbols to be added with those the Fuhrer already embraced. We were seduced by the power, the surprisingly accurate visions, and the ability to reach into the future and produce the advantage of prior knowledge and new inventions to ensure the 'new age of world order' flourished."

I felt a chill pass over my shoulders and seize my spine. It certainly sounded like Krontos could very well be this Hungarian madman mentioned in the diary. But, something was missing still. The case for his involvement wasn't airtight.

"It sounds like the writer—if it was Himmler—is lamenting the alignment, despite the advantages you listed," I said, interrupting my son's attempt to reproach Roderick for attributing something so vague to Krontos. Alistair shot me a disparaging look I ignored. "What changed the Nazis' original enthusiasm?"

"I'm glad you asked, William," said Roderick, more than willing to join me in ignoring Allistair's remarks. "From what Benevento offered, the more telling remarks occur two entries later in the diary, near the end of the chronicle. 'The Fuhrer has dissolved his relationship with the Hungarian. They parted enemies, as the madman accused us of not giving him what he wanted, insisting we had broken our promises. The demand to turn over a relic from the Jews was refused by Hitler, since the object appears to carry enough power to forge our independence from the Hungarian, and his forced allegiances to Japan and this foreigner's homeland.'"

Cedric hit a patch of ice, distracting Roderick momentarily. Once Cedric slowed down to a safer speed and Roderick was assured we wouldn't crash, he finished relating the diary's entry.

"Himmler went on to say, 'We expected a scornful response from the madman. But we were not prepared for his thorough betrayal. In early October, 1944, he began a campaign of revelations that turned the tide against us. All of our technology became known to England and the United States. Nearly every planned engagement was no longer secret. The Allies met us step for step, and the Soviets became bolder and fully assured in their aggressions. Everything has turned to shit, and news of our operations to cleanse Europe of undesirables has reached the west in much greater detail than we previously anticipated. We are in danger of losing the war and our dignity.'"

Roderick turned to face the road, leaving us to wonder if he was finished, or not.

"Well? Is that it?" asked Alistair, his tone less scornful, as if he realized he was headed for a stern lecture from me later on.

"Yes, I'm finished... for now," Roderick advised.

"So, you are assuming the relic in question is the blood coin we're after. Correct?" I asked, after the minivan settled into awkward silence. "I can see where the madman could be Krontos, though it remains a tenuous connection based on circumstantial evidence."

"I believe it's not so tenuous, William," said Roderick. "While everyone else here can be forgiven for not understanding what a full dimensional shift looks, feels, and tastes like, you and I know better."

"I fail to see where any of this proves Krontos is involved," said Alistair, his protest seconded by an emphatic nod from Amy. "I can see him being interested in the coin now that it's surfaced on the black market. But that's a far cry from claiming this asshole single-handedly turned the tide of World War II."

As much as I hated admitting the validity of Alistair's point of view, he was right. There was a lot that couldn't be proven. Hell, who's to say the diary was even written by Himmler?

"It was written by him, Judas—you're going to have to trust me, my brother," said Roderick, responding to my thoughts, and drawing quizzical looks from Alistair and Amy. "Krontos was involved with the Nazis long before he heard of this latest coin—I'm sure of it. Once he saw the opportunity to complete his vile trinity, it overrode his passion to use the Nazis to purge the world of the race he hates above all others. *Your* race, my dear friend."

"Do you believe this is true, Pops?"

Unfortunately, I did. Knew it first hand from the suffering delivered to Roderick and me nearly six hundred years ago by Krontos Lazarevic, when he had no compassion for Jews, Gypsies, and a pair of immortals who tragically crossed his path.

"Yes," I said, focusing my attention mostly on Beatrice. The look on her face announced her faith in my point of view. Amy and Alistair? Not so much. "I do, Ali."

Another 'humpf' from my kid, followed by an amused chuckle.

"Okay, Pops," he said, gesturing he was giving up the argument. "We'll just have to wait to see where this bullshit trail ends, huh?"

I wasn't sure how to respond, feeling the familiar urge to bend him over my knee and wear his butt out. Fortunately, the debate session was over, and we soon reached Auschwitz.

The initial impression was more profound than the day before. Not that any concentration camp doesn't carry a feeling of gloom and the lasting essence of evil. But those aspects hit us harder. Maybe it was the frigid conditions, or it had something to do with the forged iron sign above the entrance.

Arbeit macht frei

For those unaware, it means "Work for your freedom."

The Nazis were masters at deceit and unabashed cruelty. I have often heard observers comment on the Jewish naivety to allow themselves to be easily led to slaughter. But such comments are born from ignorance on a number of levels. For one thing, not everyone who ended up in such places was of Israelite heritage. Gypsies, gays, intellectuals, POWs and freedom fighters, and often the elite in countries offering resistance to German takeover could just as easily end up in a place like this. Although, the worse horrors of Auschwitz were

Immortal Tyranny

generally reserved for the Jews, and children of any race that ended up under Dr, Josef Mengele's 'supervision'.

I mentioned deceit and cruelty. Forgive me if you've heard this before, but for those who either skimmed over this ugly period of modern history in school, or who flat out disbelieve anything like the Holocaust could happen, I will give a quick synopsis of what life was like here. Prisoners were transported by train, stuffed in cattle cars to the point of suffocation. No food, water, or any other basic human need during transportation. Forced to sleep and relieve themselves while standing in tight quarters, some died in transport. And, for those prisoners foolishly believing death was not the ultimate goal in their being shipped to such a place as Auschwitz, that reality became crystal clear by the time they stepped off the train and were either herded to immediate slaughter in the gas chambers, or were moved to austere barracks overflowing with waiting victims whom the new arrivals would soon mimic in dress and physical condition.

Food was scarce and horrible, and yet the "Work for your freedom" edict was enforced as if the prisoners were fed to their hearts content. Eleven-hour workdays were expected, despite almost no food and stale water in limited amounts. Many died from the rigors, starvation, or were randomly killed to make a point. And for those who became too weak to meet their morning or evening roll call, an SS bayonet would either prod them out from their bunk or end their existence altogether. Severe sickness was rampant, and the gas chambers waited any and all who couldn't hold their own in this horrific environment.

Why didn't they turn and run, or allow themselves to be shot at the first sight of their oppressors? Shouldn't they all have formed militias in the ghettos and fought to an honorable death? That certainly was my initial impression from America.

It's where the deceit comes in. The millions who perished have often been referred to as 'frogs slowly boiled to death in a pot of water', meaning the indignities came slow and steady, to where Jewish and other victims were slowly desensitized to their plight and what lay ahead—a process that started years before the full extent of the Nazi agenda was made known. By the time whole neighborhoods were rounded up and shipped to the concentration camps, it was too late. Parents continuously told their children everything would be fine, scarcely believing the indignities and danger could get any worse. Then, hearing a live orchestra upon their arrival at Auschwitz to go with a large sign telling them how they could one day be free... well, you get the point. It was the final blinder to the true reality they faced, their fated roles in the Final Solution.

I could go on, but this is not intended to be a history lesson. Roderick and I didn't lecture Amy, Alistair, and Beatrice on any of this, as they quietly moved through the cold memorial-museum that is Auschwitz. Cedric had been here shortly after the Iron Curtain came down, and seemed ready to leave soon after we began our tour. This time, Roderick led the way, and I followed.

"What is that smell?" asked Amy, wiping at her nose as we moved to the row of barracks. Alistair's response was similar.

"It's the lingering residue from burnt hair and flesh," offered Cedric, solemnly. "It was stronger the last time I was here, in 1996. It seems to get weaker over time, but sure as shit it's still there, man. It'll mess with your mind as you explore the grounds, realizing Nazi cruelty still lingers in the air seventy years after the war ended."

Beatrice squeezed my hand, as if to remind me to stay close. I wrapped my arm around her shoulder to pull her against me, and I caught her grateful smile as she glanced up at

Immortal Tyranny

my face. Alistair pulled Amy close, and we followed Cedric who picked up his pace to catch up with Roderick.

It wasn't until we began moving through the third barrack that I noticed Roderick was silently crying. All of us were overwhelmed by sadness, but the initial tears at Stutthof softened the worse emotional blows from this place that saw more than a million victims lose their lives.

"Are you getting anything?" I asked him, gently.

He shook his head, and at first couldn't respond verbally.

"How about you?" he whispered, once able.

"Nothing," I said, pursing my lips in frustration. I had seen a slight blue glow in the second barracks, but that was it.

"They weren't here long enough," said Roderick, dabbing at his eyes with a handkerchief. "I had the impression of surprise, and I think it might be from Simon Lieberman. I sense he was alone from the start, and his parents were taken immediately to the gas chambers…. He didn't know what to do, and held on to the coin in fear of someone trying to take it from him—like the girl back in Stutthof."

Roderick sniffed and swiftly moved to the barrack's exit.

"What, are we leaving?" Alistair asked him, his tone surprisingly compassionate. "We haven't seen one fourth of this place yet. Pops… well, are you going to stop him or not?"

"I'll be right back," I said, immediately pursuing Roderick.

I feared he might've run to where our rental was parked. But he hadn't exited the camp yet.

"Do you wish to tell me what's going on?"

"I can't do this," he said, softly. "I knew I should never come here again. I had no idea what could happen if I came here focused on one individual…."

"Simon Lieberman?" I carefully prodded, when he refused to go on, shaking his head defiantly as he gritted his teeth.

"I'm so sorry, Judas," he said, motioning behind me. Everyone else was on the way to meet us. "I will tell you this quickly, and then I want to forget about this place and what happened here. Okay?"

"All right."

I glanced over my shoulder. He had about thirty seconds... maybe a minute. Alistair was dragging behind the group, and like dominos, Amy, Beatrice, and Cedric stopped to wait for him.

"Simon was lost, so heartbroken from the loss of his parents," said Roderick. "Keep in mind he thought he had lost his sister at Stutthof. He became desperate to get out, though there was no way he could leave. That's the impression I'm getting.... The boy foolishly tried to bribe a guard who had befriended him—likely in hope of eventual sexual favors. But seeing the silver shekel and its strange glow, though faint, was how it left Simon Lieberman's possession. Once the kid and his family's coin were brought to Richard Baer, the commandant confiscated the coin and forced the guard to put a bullet in Simon's head."

It took me nearly half an hour to console Roderick. Not since the loss of his wife and child roughly seventeen hundred years ago had I seen him this grief stricken. That's all I needed to effectively keep my son and anyone else from badgering him with questions as we took our journey one step further than originally anticipated.

"What in the hell is in Budapest?" asked Cedric, as we headed to Slovakia, with our destiny one country further south in Hungary. We would reach our destination by nightfall, provided the weather didn't worsen.

"You mean, *who* in the hell is in Budapest," I corrected him, playfully. Well, playfully as the overall somber mood in the minivan could tolerate. "We're going to visit Krontos."

Immortal Tyranny

"*Huh?!* Pops have you lost your frigging mind?!"

Alistair's scorn was understandable, and everyone but Roderick had similar reactions. Alistair and Amy shared the back seat once more, and I rejoined Beatrice in the middle, where she suddenly clamped her hands around my left forearm as if hanging on for dear life. Her eyes were filled with fear, and for a moment I wondered if somewhere deep inside her psyche the terrible experience she had endured at Dracul's castle lingered, like a distant memory from a past life. Only in this case, it was her current life until Krontos changed the script.

Her terror notwithstanding, we had no choice.

"We must go to Hungary and end this tyranny," said Roderick, his voice echoing around us, but subdued. If I didn't know better, I'd say he was afflicted with some sort of sickness, which is damned near impossible for an immortal that has lived beyond several hundred years. "He is there. The impression is coming to me in the same manner I've received every other image and insight the past two days."

"So, Krontos is in Budapest, Hungary, and we are on our way to casually drop in, huh?" Amy sounded like Alistair, and it was difficult to not picture them as a GQ pair of Hummels. Or, if I were a fairy tale wicked witch, Hansel and Gretel. "What happens if he's just a tad irritated that we are here and not waiting for him in Sedona, as instructed?"

Good point, and something I had seriously considered. But after so many years of avoiding this little old man with the Napoleonic complex, it was time to settle things once and for all. To 'end the tyranny', as Roderick aptly stated.

"Krontos likely suffers from the same malady of being stuck in or near his castle, as Dracul was," I said. "If it's the same one we last strolled by in… what was the year, Rod?"

"1796, when I came to see you in England, and we traveled to Turkey to visit the St. Germain brothers."

"Ah, yes, that was it," I said. "But that particular castle was in the Mátra Mountains, about ninety-seven kilometers from Budapest."

Cedric eyed me suspiciously in the rearview mirror, until Roderick assured him that we wouldn't travel to the castle before morning.

"I knew when we visited Stutthof yesterday that we would be going to Hungary in search of Krontos," Roderick confessed. "The sensation in my 'heart of hearts' told me then what was confirmed at Auschwitz today. Krontos has been operating all this time from the castle. That is why he has procured the local mafia, to be his arms and legs, and depending on the circumstances, his voice. They do his bidding, and as William and I experienced in Budva, Krontos can possess unwitting human subjects to give a message."

The response from our companions was predictably guarded. Cedric was absent, and the others had their memories wiped clean by Krontos changing the sequence of events when they came to look for Roderick and me. It's too much to explain here, if anyone missed hearing about it. But I detailed it fairly thoroughly in my previous journal.

"But, you said Krontos is not a vampire," said Amy, distrust in her tone. "Why would he be stuck? From what you and Roderick have repeatedly stated, Krontos is a master at controlling time and space."

"No, he can't control space," Roderick corrected her. "Just time and dimensions, since space indicates untamed chaos beyond our solar system. Do you follow me?" He waited for her response, a slight nod. "Krontos may possess genius the world has not seen before, but he still follows scientific principles, or laws. And, he is not an anarchist. Even when we were acquaintances on peaceful terms, when he posed as a French aristocrat before the revolution, he never wanted to watch the world burn. Rather, he has always desired to control it, and ultimately conform it to his vision."

Whether or not he made the point he sought with her remained to be seen. She cuddled with Alistair, and they both kept a watchful eye on him, until he grew uncomfortable and returned his view to the flurried road ahead of us. The storm seemed to have the same destination we did.

"William, what do you think of this compromise," said Roderick, keeping his focus on the road while Cedric deftly navigated through treacherous ice patches. "If by tomorrow morning, Beatrice, Amy, or Alistair come up with a reason strong enough to override yours and my conviction to press on to the Mátra Mountains, we will immediately head back to Berlin and fly home Monday afternoon. Otherwise, we stay the course until it is no longer prudent to hunt Krontos. Agreed?"

The last part sounded like Cedric's words from the other night. Meanwhile, I couldn't think of a reason strong enough to call off this potentially foolhardy trip and head back to Germany. Nothing that could override Roderick's conviction. But the bigger question was the same one we started with two nights ago. How would we, or *could* we, ever know if we were being manipulated by Krontos to come to Hungary… or not?

Impossible to answer, and at least for me, the question promised another restless night.

Chapter Eleven

"What about our flight home from Berlin?" worried Beatrice, shortly after we settled in our room at the Hotel Victoria in Budapest. "Tomorrow is Halloween, which leaves us only two more days to make it back in time for our flight. What if something goes wrong and we are delayed, or worse?"

"If there is a delay, I'll take care of it," I told her, pausing to give her a reassuring hug and kiss. "The important thing is to take every precaution as we travel into the mountains."

"He knows we're coming, doesn't he?"

Her eyes glistened as the depth of her worry surfaced.

"Yes... I believe he does."

What else could I say? Krontos had known our every move for at least the past five months, and more likely, since our return from Bolivia last November. Stating the truth, as I've understood it, has always been the best way to go. I smiled, hoping to reassure her while I reflected on this lesson—one that my beloved wife had a hand in teaching me.

"Are we walking into a trap?"

"You mean driving into a trap."

"William!" she scolded. "You *know* what I meant!"

"I think 'trap' is a strong word to use at this point," I said, mustering every ounce of positive energy within me to keep my smile and countenance radiant. "We need answers only Krontos can provide. I think it's the same thing Roderick believes. Despite your misgivings, you can't tell me part of you doesn't feel inexplicably drawn to a meeting on his turf. Despite the danger we all fear, each of us is being pulled to Krontos like moths to a flame."

"I think we're all nervous," she said. " I feel something... but calling it attraction to an evil man who is just as apt to kill us as give answers seems a bit stretched, don't you think?"

Count on my better half to cut through the bullshit and get to the heart of the matter. Despite the pull to Hungary and

Roderick's and my anticipated first face-to-face encounter with Krontos in nearly two hundred and twenty years, something about this situation felt wrong. Hell, it felt absurd, and if I knew of a place where we could all safely hide indefinitely, we'd be on the way there now.

What if Krontos wasn't there when we found his ancient castle? What if he had sold the place or moved on, letting it fall into ruin—with no sign of him anywhere? We couldn't find anything like it when we tried to drill down into Google maps from Roderick's computer earlier that afternoon. So, anything was possible.

I suddenly worried about Krontos not being in Hungary, perhaps seeking to uncover the hiding place for my coins in Sedona. All but one lay buried there. The Dragon Coin was the only coin making the trip with us, securely wrapped and placed inside my wallet.

A knock on the door interrupted our discussion.

"Pops? Mother? ...Cedric and Roderick are down in the lobby, waiting on us to go to dinner," Alistair advised, from outside our door.

"We're coming, Ali. Just give us a moment," I called to him.

"Promise me you won't do anything foolish, due to your hatred of this fiend Krontos," urged Beatrice. "Don't put you or any of us in harm's way."

"I don't hate him—"

"Pops—we haven't got all night!"

We would have to continue this discussion later. I grabbed our coats and gently nudged her toward the door. Alistair and Amy seemed pleased to see us, and more refreshed after parting company less than thirty minutes earlier.

"It sounds like we might finally have a good time on this trip," said Alistair, as we walked to the nearest elevator.

"Roderick has booked our dinner reservations at the oldest inn in town, the Százéves Étterem. He said he came here shortly after World War II, right before Stalin completed his Iron Curtain."

"There will be live music, too!" Amy enthused.

I hoped their merrier moods proved to be a lasting thing, even if only through tonight.

Roderick and Cedric were waiting downstairs, and seemed refreshed. I had worried Cedric might need an early start to a good night's rest when we arrived at the hotel, due to the rigors of driving all day. But the opulent appointments and flirtatious desk clerk who checked us in seemed to revive his spirits. As for Roderick, I think he was relieved to not need as much primping to get his slightly bronzed look back. Despite the anguish he endured at Auschwitz, the previous afternoon's excursion to Stutthof had taken a greater physical toll, and left his pallid complexion fully exposed when we arrived in Krakow. Not so tonight.

"So, you decided on a visit to Százéves Étterem after all," I teased Roderick. "And here I thought you might want to try someplace new."

He chuckled and led the way out of the hotel. A frigid gust greeted us as we headed for our rental.

"It seemed like the best choice," he said, while all of us jogged to the minivan. "Something with a little local flavor, history, and the best Gypsy music in town."

Sounded like fun. Especially seeing my wife's countenance light up. Beatrice needed this as much as anyone else. The restaurant was packed, and yet the revelry with strangers was refreshing for me. I, too, was able to forget the sorrow and sense of loss that had followed us from the concentration camp museum-memorials we visited. Finally able to push Krontos and his wicked schemes from my immediate awareness, I began to relax.

We stayed at the restaurant until ten o'clock, after all of us had enjoyed nearly three hours of great food, drink, and uproarious fun. I offered to join Roderick in retrieving our ride, since Cedric was seriously inebriated. The feeling of merriment followed us past the portico. But like the arctic breezes that had assaulted us throughout the day, an ominous sensation overwhelmed my senses. Then the source feeding my sudden trepidation appeared before us, stepping into the glow from the nightspot's neon sign, near where our vehicle waited.

"Ah, we meet again, Judas and Roderick!" announced the familiar blonde, blue-eyed man dressed in a dark trench coat. Arso Dmitar, whom we last encountered as one of Vlad Tepes' henchmen, approached us, flicking a glowing cigarette butt into a small snowdrift beneath a nearby juniper bush. Flanked by two other men we recognized, Jevrem and Gajo, it was obvious this wasn't a benign social call. "We've been expecting you."

Hard to say why we said nothing, choosing to retreat to where the others stood, just outside the entrance. After all, we had bested this trio of Dracul's thugs in Budva, sending them scurrying away. Of course, that was before they reappeared as helpful guides to Alistair, Amy, and Beatrice when the reality shift occurred as Roderick and I stepped out of the Adriatic Sea. Obviously, they worked for a new employer now, and likely the same one back then: Krontos Lazarevic.

Alistair and Amy waved to the three men stealthily approaching the crowded entrance to Százéves Étterem, as if they were long lost friends. Gajo raised his chin in a subtle greeting, his dark eyes and slicked-back black hair glistening in the soft neon glow. Jevrem's dark, loosened locks were as preened as Arso's. The trio looked like a heavy metal act carrying musical instruments beneath their coats, though a surer bet was automatic weapons lay hidden instead—either small rifles or pistols. Were they sent by Krontos to cut us down?

"Quick! Get back inside!"

"Huh?! Pops, what in the hell—"

"Just do as I say, son—you, too, Amy!"

I shoved them toward the door, along with a gentler push to Beatrice, shaking my head when she sought an explanation. Meanwhile, Roderick grabbed Cedric and coerced him inside the restaurant.

I prayed we weren't endangering innocent patrons, and I banked on the fact these guys likely bore familiarity, and could easily be identified—regardless of the immortal menace supporting them.

"It's useless to run, Judas!" Arso called after us. I believe he said something after that, but whatever additional warning he uttered was absorbed by the din of music and noisy patrons singing and dancing inside.

I hoped to go deeper into the restaurant, toward an exit I noticed earlier, not far from our table. But I ran into Roderick. He had stopped, and once I saw what he was looking at, I stopped, too. Stopped, while wearing a stunned expression.

"What the hell?" said Cedric, slurring his words, as he pointed to a small bar, and a much smaller room than we had reveled in just minutes ago. "Where did everybody go?"

"Are we in the right area? Maybe we came in a side entrance and this is another side of the restaurant," said Amy, her calm tone belied by her nonplussed look.

"Damn it!" hissed Roderick. "He's already changed everything! There's *nowhere* to go!"

Nowhere, but back from whence we just came.

Immortal Tyranny

Beatrice clung tightly to me as I turned toward the entrance we had stepped through, less than thirty feet away. I expected to see the three Budva hoodlums waiting smugly inside the doorway. Maybe even with their weapons drawn, held above their heads and pointed to the ceiling like famed miscreants Pancho Villa or John Dillinger. But the threesome was absent, apparently waiting outside.

Or, maybe in some other dimension?

I ignored the fear building rapidly inside me, instead relying on reason to assess the situation and determine the smartest move. A move necessitating much more wisdom than any of us had demonstrated since leaving Sedona, Arizona.

"Well, can either of you tell us what the hell is going on here?" Alistair asked, shifting his gaze from Roderick to me, and then back again. "Maybe our friends outside can enlighten us, since the two of you are absolutely no help!"

Alistair took a step toward the door. Amy reached out and grabbed his arm.

"Don't Ali," she said softly, her eyes pleading. "It's all wrong!"

"What? Now *you*, too?"

"She's right, son," I agreed, reaching to stop him from pulling away from her grasp. "It's *all* wrong."

"I'm afraid there's no other choice, other than stepping through that door," said Roderick, shaking his head wearily as he moved toward the exit.

I couldn't stop them both. Beatrice increased her grip on my arm, her eyes tightly closed. Meanwhile, something new was happening. Patrons who made warm eye contact upon our arrival now regarded us warily. Was it Krontos at work? I tried to think of something other than what was happening. I thought about our trip, the hotel, Auschwitz—anything to not let my mind wander aimlessly. A non-purposeful mind seemed to be the prescription for a Hungarian mentalist takeover.

I pictured Roderick holding the same resolve. But, if so, he chose an entirely different way to express it. He picked up his pace and exploded through the main door, with Alistair, Cedric, Amy, and soon Beatrice and me behind him.

A silver Mercedes SUV sat waiting for us at the edge of the sidewalk. The vehicle's passenger doors open, Arso and Jevrem beckoned for us to get in. The pompous blonde eyed me knowingly, after offering a similar smirk to Roderick.

"It is useless to resist," Arso advised, his Slavic accent more pronounced than earlier. "Not to mention, it is better not to keep the Master waiting."

CHAPTER TWELVE

Immortal Tyranny

Traveling with these goons was surreal—especially when Alistair and Amy bantered with Jevrem and Arso. Beatrice politely commented when our son and his fiancée drew her into the conversation. A conversation, I might add, involving the sightseeing trip the three thugs escorted my family on, while in another reality they were assisting Dracul in his attempts to end Roderick's and my earthly existence.

"Where are you taking us?" Cedric blurted out, when the initial shallowness gave way to awkward silence. He was still hammered, though obviously aware of the dangerous turn our evening on the town had taken.

"Well... let's just say we have been instructed to save you a trip to the Mátra Mountains," said Arso, chuckling and nodding to his cohorts, as if this was some private joke. "I regret to inform you this will not be a scenic trip, as it might have been had you driven into the mountains tomorrow morning as planned. Besides, snow is in the forecast tonight."

He motioned to wet flakes pelting the windshield. Arso sat in the front passenger seat, and Jevrem sat behind him, next to Amy and Alistair. Roderick and Cedric sat in front of Beatrice and me, as we sat in the very back of the vehicle damned near as big as our rented minivan. Gajo was the driver, reminiscent of when Roderick and I traveled with these guys to Dracul's castle the past June. Fitting, since the guy rarely spoke.

"Who told you we were coming tomorrow?" I asked. "Krontos?"

"Why, of course," said Arso, his warm tone slightly icier.

"I suppose we should be flattered he cared enough to send you guys to pick us up," said Roderick. "Sounds like he's anxious to see us."

Words I might've offered in the past. Roderick's subtle taunt brought a slight smile to my face... until I saw the latest dread in Beatrice's eyes.

Immortal Tyranny

"Don't flatter yourselves, yet," said Jevrem, evenly. "Master has not been pleased by your disdain for his warnings."

"Is that why he went to the trouble of eliminating the competition in Berlin?" I asked, cheerfully, adding a shit-eating grin I hoped these guys could detect in the car's dimness. "And here I thought he ruled the world uncontested."

"Watch your tongue, Judas!" Arso snapped. "Unless you want a less than cordial greeting when we arrive at our destination, you would be wise to shut the hell up!"

"Aren't we touchy." I chuckled while Beatrice tensed next to me. "By the way, has Krontos upgraded to a new swanky pad, or does he still prefer the medieval dinginess we last visited in... when was it again, Roderick?"

"Seventeen-ninety-six," said Roderick, wearily. He hadn't anticipated where I was going with this, but played along. "And, yes, Judas... we were on our way to visit Comte and Raccczis de St. Germain."

"I'm impressed," said Arso, snickering. "You both once knew the infamous St. Germain brothers? How clever."

"Do you know how old your 'master' is?" I asked him, while everyone other than Roderick surely wondered what in the hell this thread had to do with anything pertinent to our present circumstances. When he simply glared in my direction, I pressed him further. "No? You wouldn't even hazard a guess, Arso? Last I checked, you were telling my druid companion and me the two of you shared sorcery skills. Skills that should tell you how long the little old man ruling the world from inside his shit-hole in the Mátra Mountains has been at the game. No guess at all?"

"Judas... let it go," pleaded Roderick. Hell, Beatrice, Amy, and Alistair wore mortified looks to match his entreaty. Only

Cedric looked amused, likely wondering if a full-on fight was coming while his buzz continued to wane. "He's just a kid."

Nice. An unexpected barb that successfully hit a nerve. Even from where I sat, I could tell Arso's complexion was heating from anger. Very nice, Roderick!

"Your 'master' was soiling his infant garments by the time both of us—and the St. Germain brothers—had been walking the earth for a few centuries past our first millennium," I continued, praying my kid especially remained lock-jawed in surprise, and more importantly, silent. "Rod, what do most historians agree was the birth date for Krontos Lazarevic?"

"There are several dates that have been proposed over the years, the most popular being thirteen-twenty-six, A.D."

I couldn't see Roderick's expression, but his matter-of-fact tone told me he was completely in tune with what I tried to achieve.

"And, yet, these clowns knew none of this," I said, allowing a stronger chuckle than before. "I guess they don't teach much history in Hungarian schools, or what passes for education in Montenegro, eh?"

"You, shut the hell up!" shouted Jevrem, reaching for the gun concealed in his coat. "Maybe you would like to join your American friend and the German traitor in a river! Is that what you want, asshole?!"

Bingo.

So, we had confirmation as to who killed Thomas Wilburn and Franz Reifenstahl. One less thing for Krontos to play with, should he seek to shift our reality.

I was beginning to develop a theory about the rules surrounding Krontos' ability to alter dimensions. Knowledge shared with others might prevent a shift. Yeah, it sounds almost as crazy as the ability to alter reality. But, consider a few interesting facts before dismissing the idea of how knowledge might affect Krontos' power. Roderick and I shared a reality in Dracul's castle that remained intact throughout—while Beatrice, Alistair, and Amy had the experience wiped clean and replaced with another. Yet, Roderick and I had virtually nothing wiped. Other than our shared immortal status, what else did we have in common? Nothing. Only the continuous confirmation of the reality we dealt with. Namely, that we were facing death, and never stopped reminding each other about what we were up against. Perhaps the induced strain was another factor.

Even if my theory were eventually foiled, knowing what happened to Agent Wilburn was important. As long as Jevrem didn't shoot the two of us, or our family.

"Hey, man, I wasn't trying to upset you."

"Bullshit, Judas!" shouted Arso.

Maybe I did push too hard.

"Look, sorry I was a bit crass," I confessed. "But, if Krontos wants any cooperation from me, the three of you will need to play nice. Otherwise, I'll lock down tighter than an iron chastity belt, and he can take out his frustration on each of you instead. How does that sound?"

The tension didn't immediately abate, and surely everyone but Roderick thought I had lost my frigging mind by continuing to be an ass. Even he looked nervous as Arso and Jevrem pointed Russian assault rifles at us.

"AN-94's, both modified," Roderick mused softly. His tone was steady and detached. "Impressive."

"Well, we could go on about how your Russian neighbors still build superior guns compared to your local gunsmiths, but I believe you guys are far too sensitive to handle such a discussion." I kept my tone merry and confident, too deep in this shit to back out meekly. *That* alone could get us riddled with bullets. Cold-blooded killers such as this trio were like sharks, and unlikely to resist a frenzied feast upon frightened blood—their boss's imminent displeasure notwithstanding. "Why not put your toys away, before you end up angering the sorcerer who created your last employer, Dracul?"

It was dicey, and perhaps stupid. Certainly there are those out there who would view this latest reckless endangerment of my beloved wife and son—hell, all four mortals—as cause for a stern rebuke. But it wasn't like we were going to grandmother's house for Sunday dinner. For all any of us knew, Krontos might well be waiting in the castle driveway, ready to snatch one of the AN-94's from either Arso or Jevrem and himself mow us down in a shower of bullets.

In my defense, and based upon my lengthy experience in life, engendering tension among one's captors has often resulted in me and my allies gaining the upper hand. Arlo and Jevrem slowly lowered their weapons as the debate within raged on, until they finally returned them to the holsters inside their coats.

"We shall see what Krontos decides," said Arlo, his tone frigid. "Maybe he will let us participate in your coercion, should you continue to prove difficult to deal with, Judas. If so, we will start with your son and his girlfriend, and move on to your beautiful wife. Only if necessary, of course."

He smiled meanly, letting his dead blue eyes linger on each of us before turning his attention back to the road ahead. Jevrem soon followed suit, and neither one spoke a word until we reached the mountains. From that point on, Arlo spoke occasionally by radio to someone else, using an unfamiliar Slavic dialect. Likely one of the older regional dialects. My guess was Krontos taught it to his subjects to keep his dealings with his staff undecipherable to outsiders.

The Mercedes eventually veered onto a narrow two-lane highway that took us up a mountainside. Near the top, stood

Immortal Tyranny

the castle of Krontos Lazarevic. Though it had fallen on hard times back by 1796, which made me openly wonder if it was still standing, the fully restored magisterial structure glistened beneath the clear light from a crescent moon. Many of the castle's rooms were aglow, and for the moment it was impossible to tell if the lamps were candle, gas, or electric.

"Or aglow by his very will," said Roderick, glancing at me after barging in on my private musing.

Beatrice shuddered and drew nearer to me, and I pulled her close to shelter her. Amy scooted closer to Alistair, while Cedric subtly shook his head. Meanwhile, our escorts looked worried, as if they had time to digest my warnings to them, and actually believed it possible that Krontos would be displeased by their behavior. Gajo coasted past an immense marble fountain featuring Poseidon in its center, dormant for the moment, and brought the vehicle to a halt before the main entrance.

An entourage of butlers, footmen, and maidservants, dressed similarly to the last time we were here, lined both sides of the granite steps leading to the door that lay open. The staff bowed and curtseyed as we all exited the Mercedes, flanked by Arlo and Jevrem, while Gajo followed behind us. I could see the shadow from his rifle, as if he expected us to flee.

"As they say in America, 'Here goes nothin'!'" whispered Roderick, smiling slightly as he led the way up the steps.

Indeed. Perhaps the phrase "Something from nothing will leave you nothing in the end" would be even more apropos. After all, we were dealing with a sorcerer. A sorcerer who knew the secrets of time, dimensional travel, and how to distort reality.

Immortal Tyranny

CHAPTER THIRTEEN

Immortal Tyranny

My heart pounded heavily as we stepped into the castle's grand foyer. When Roderick and I last stopped here, admittedly it was to gloat at Krontos' ill health. He had somehow ingested an unknown poison. Shamed now that we took solace in this monster's likely death, we assumed it would happen soon after we viewed his writhing body lying on what amounted to a makeshift, surgical table.

Like a vampire seized by blood sickness after drinking from a dead body, the poison caused Krontos' gray eyes to flood crimson—more hideous than the ink-like appearance his eyes would take on in a fit of rage. I would've given whoever felled this fiend a handsome sum for taking out one of the cruelest tormentors I had dealt with in my near eighteen-hundred-year-old existence back then. Roderick had suffered nearly as much. If he had died, I might have sought to torture Krontos on his deathbed, severely.

But we left him in his filth, ignoring his pleas for mercy and to find a certain berry that grew wild in these mountains. It was the thing he claimed could heal his sickness. His servant staff had deserted him—likely because of frequent ill-tempered attacks, both verbally and physically.

As to who had done the deed, we never found out. Rumor reached me in England two years later that Krontos had recovered from his illness and set out to find the wench who tried to end his life. Nearly ninety years later, when Roderick came to visit me in London, and before Ratibor was revealed to be Jack The Ripper, I considered Krontos to be the culprit—largely from what we heard he had done to the woman who had tried to kill him. The anger driving her to find a poison that would work on this ancient alchemist turned out to be nothing in comparison to the vengeful rage inspiring him to visit a dozen countries in two continents to find her.

I shuddered as I considered the report on what the police in Brussels found. Only a locket and her status as a previously arrested prostitute served to identify the corpse brutally torn from the inside out.

"Greetings Judas and Roderick! Welcome to you, Beatrice, Alistair, Amy, and Cedric!"

The timber of the voice familiar, the power causing it to echo against the foyer's marble walls and beyond was not. A diminutive figure approached us from the castle's depths. Dressed in a black robe with the hood pulled back, the lustrous white hair falling onto the figure's shoulders and the pale gray eyes should have identified who it was. But the slight limp—something he entered eternal life with—confirmed Krontos' purposeful approach. A much more comely and vibrant version of this immortal than we had encountered before, we faced a difficult task reconciling the vile history with the charisma attendant now.

"You look as if you've seen a ghost, Judas," he said, upon reaching where we stood, just inside the foyer.

Alistair and Amy were busy admiring the ring of stained glass windows high above, along with an incredible fresco. More impressive in detail than the ceiling we had seen in the Essene's Bolivian residence, this one appeared to have been done by an actual master. That's what Beatrice murmured.

"Annibale Carracci is the artist," Krontos announced, proudly. "The scene should be one familiar to you, Judas."

The betrayal portrayals I had previously seen were nowhere near as flattering as this one, although it still was far from accurate. Very few artists have caught the essence of what happened that night in Gethsemane, and later at Simon Zelotes' palatial home.

"If you had not been in such a hurry to leave me stranded when you and Roderick stopped by on your way to Istanbul, you might have seen this magnificent work by Carracci!" Krontos enthused. He offered a generous smile. Even his veneers glistened, or the illusion of veneers if what we viewed with our eyes wasn't actually there. "But, why waste time on old wounds and injustices? I committed them, too. How I long to move on from our past, and let bygones be bygones."

The warmth and jovial air were unexpected. Roderick's perplexed expression confirmed he had the same reaction. Perhaps a tongue-lashing, or worse, was still coming. But for the moment, the warmth in Krontos' smile and cheerful voice seemed genuine.

I searched my memory for anything to hint our long awaited reunion would be like this. The last time we had seen the bastard in full health was at a ball, the last one held by Marie Antoinette. Shouting vicious curses at a young peasant woman and her starving child lingering by the palace gates at Versailles.... His eyes back then were black as midnight—as dark as any vampire or other soulless creature Roderick and I had ever laid eyes on.

Impossible to reconcile that image with the man standing before us. Even as he chastised us for coming to Hungary, instead of staying put in Arizona, he did so with merriment in his tone... and, dare I say, compassion?

"If I needed you or your coin, I could have taken either or both at any time—you know this by now, no?" said Krontos, chuckling as he led us into a large reception area. The room was opulent as the foyer and grand staircase we passed along the way. Several female servants stood to either side of the room, carrying hot cider and cocoa. All of us waived off the refreshments when approached. "Do not fear me, my friends. I intend you no harm."

Of course, none of us took a sip until Krontos gulped down half a glass of each beverage.

"There... you see? I am still well as you all will be. Drink. Surely you are thirsty and cold within."

"Perhaps. But you have always been a cunning sorcerer, Krontos," said Roderick. "Very few of the world's poisons can harm you."

"And that makes me evil, then?"

He laughed, and the mirthful look in his eyes was soft and cheerful. I felt a chill cross my spine as the image of Josef Mengele came to mind, fresh from that afternoon. Like Krontos, Auschwitz' famed wicked doctor was outwardly kind, too. And, look what happened to the Jews and Gypsies who trusted him—especially the children to whom he offered fatherly comfort.

"I'm just a silent observer, watching the world and its deceitful ways, Judas," he said, undeterred by the silence and suspicious gazes surrounding him. "And, talk about deceit. How is that coin collecting pursuit of yours working out? I do believe you are slowing down, old boy. Obviously, you are in no hurry to finish and leave this world when your wife and child are so young once again. Hmmmm.... Perhaps I should try your crystals, eh?"

What could I say in response? Especially while sorting through the latest mindfuck. Krontos played as if he had access to my thoughts... or was it just a masterful salesman reading his prey?

"Why don't you take out your wallet, William-Judas, and see if the Dragon Coin remains there. You have long feared me taking it back, so why not check to make sure it's still there?"

I did fear it. In fact, I spent much of the journey into the mountains trying to think of an effective hiding place, should it become necessary. I fished out my wallet from my pants, and without showing everyone else, determined the coin was still

Immortal Tyranny

there. Wrapped in cerecloth, I only revealed one exposed side in my wallet. The coin was glowing blue.

Roderick saw the coin's radiance, and no doubt, so did Krontos. I was certain no one else could see it. I suddenly worried Krontos could figure out where the other twenty-four collected coins were at present. I tried to think of obscure places and things to prevent him from connecting the dots from my other thoughts to reveal exactly where the other coins lay hidden.

"Well, is it there?" he persisted, his loving smile never wavering.

"Yes. It's there."

I closed my wallet and returned it to my pocket, wondering if the coin would still be there when I checked again, later on.

"Good. I would offer you supper, but I understand you have eaten already. Perhaps you would like to retire to your rooms, since we will begin our reclamation project in the morning," Krontos advised.

"So, you won't allow us to return to our own lodging arrangements?" asked Roderick.

"Oh, I'm sorry," Krontos replied, chuckling. "And, here I thought you came all this way to Budapest to keep me company. How foolish of me to assume so."

"We came to find out why you killed off the competition for the Stuthoff-Auschwitz coin," I said, purposely not acknowledging his 'Holocaust' label for the coin.

"An answer to the question and you'll be on your way then? Is that any way to treat an old friend you have not visited in more than two centuries?" Krontos continued to smile, but his tone bore a slight chill. He moved over to one of the servants and picked up a fresh cup of cocoa before continuing. "You assume this is the truth, Judas. We have much to discuss about the very event you mentioned… but not tonight."

115

"Why not tonight? For one thing, we're not friends," I said, feeling my blood begin to boil. "Friends don't try to kill each other. Nor do they send threatening notes."

"Hmmm… yes, that is unfortunate," he said, his smile fading as his brow furrowed. As if he was deeply pained by the accusation. But just as quickly as his countenance turned cloudy, his warm smile returned. "Let bygones become bygones, Judas and Roderick. I intend no harm to you, your family, and your friends. Why not stay tonight and hear my proposition of peace to you at breakfast? What would Beatrice, Alistair, Amy, and Cedric like to do? Stay here and enjoy the amenities, or go back to your hotel in Budapest with the intent to travel back here tomorrow and spy on my castle as originally planned—something I already knew about and had a plan to thwart? It's obvious which option makes the most sense."

True. Although, where was the assurance he wouldn't have his thugs or house servants slip into our rooms and slit our throats? Or, serve some sort of poison in a clever manner undetectable by Roderick or me?

Krontos drained his cup and motioned for the girl he took it from to take it back. Then, he returned from whence he came, shaking his head in disappointment.

"You may do as you like," he called to us, once he left the room. "Gajo will take you back to Budapest, and we will let the matter end here. Or, you can accept my hospitality and be in position to recover the coin you seek. Should you decide to stay the night, Alida and Eneh will show you to your rooms. Good evening."

As unprepared for this response as we had been for the entire encounter with Krontos, we all watched him continue to walk away until the shrouded little Hungarian became too indistinct to follow. Roderick spoke first.

"It feels like a trap. However, I get the feeling he truly needs our help."

"Doing what?" asked Alistair.

"My thought exactly, Ali," I said. "If we leave, we might never know what it is he needs help with. And, it's not like we can study the place from a safe distance and figure out why we were drawn here in the first place...."

I felt like a complete fool as realization set in that we had been played. Expertly so? Not necessarily. But by virtue of bringing us here—subtly from Germany and blatantly that night—it was too late to retake control of a situation we likely never had such power in the first place. Definitely not since our arrival in Berlin. Hell, the cheese-filled maze could've been started when we decided to take matters into our own hands in Sedona... and possibly even before then.

There was no way to know anything for certain anymore.

"The safest option is to stay," said Cedric, who had been surveying our surroundings since we stepped into the castle, as if he were searching for camouflaged sniper points. Old CIA habits die hard. "That's what my gut tells me, Willie Boy. I bet that's what Roderick's instincts would say, too, if this was the covert deal we handled thirty years ago in Croatia. Remember that, man? We weren't dealing with a sorcerer, but those cats were smarter than Washington expected. It's the same deal here, and had we stayed put once things got really jacked up, we'd have been better off—"

"You made your point," Roderick interrupted him. "We'll stay."

A joyless resolution, Beatrice and Amy carried the most misgivings. But in the end, we all agreed our options were limited. The promise of favorable accommodations in the castle won out over a two-hour journey back to a hotel that might not be as familiar as it had been when we left for dinner.

It was the only logical assumption to make as long as Krontos was in control.

Chapter Fourteen

Immortal Tyranny

As had become my habit during this trip, I didn't sleep. Instead, I kept a protective eye on Beatrice as she slept, her well being my greatest concern. I worried about Alistair and Amy's welfare, too, in the assigned room next to ours. But I took comfort in the fact I heard my son's snores when I slipped away for a moment to press my ear against their door. It left only Roderick and Cedric to worry about, and I counted on them both keeping a vigil where light sleep was all they managed.

"We can't let him downplay our shared past, my brother," said Roderick, who must have sensed my presence in the hallway. I moved away from the door in fear my son or Amy might hear me, and steered us both away from the room I shared with Beatrice for the same reason. "Above all things, Krontos is a *liar!*"

The beginning of a half hour conversation where we relived the injustices wrought against us. What brought the greatest anger was the fact this wicked bastard had enabled two bloodthirsty men to attain significant reigns of murder, mayhem, and cruelty that pushed the limits of mankind's immorality. Dracul, better known as Vlad the Impaler, and Adolf Hitler. Were they mere puppets disguising the designs of a hidden tyrant whose lust for human conquest far exceeded their own?

Thousands were killed by the Inquisition, as Dracul pretended to be a leading Cardinal championing the punishment of infidels. This came after a lifetime of butchering enemies as the legendary Prince of Wallachia—at least half of the estimated one hundred thousand victims were impaled. Of course, this was a mere pittance in comparison to the millions who died under Hitler's efforts to purge undesirables while seeking to establish a new world order. A world order that was

Krontos' second attempt to subject the earth's residents to his depraved imaginations.

Would the third time be a charm?

It wasn't hard to picture a new Final Solution, and the victims might not be chosen by race or nationality. Maybe this time it would be kindred ideologies that would either survive or be purged. The only thing known for certain was Krontos' ruthlessness. A dangerous man and immortal in years past, he was more so now, as long as he held all the cards. It was far easier picturing him crushing the throats of my star-marked brethren seventy years ago with Nazi boot heels than to believe his current amicable disposition was a lasting thing….

"How did you sleep?" asked Krontos, at breakfast, maintaining the same damned giddiness from the night before. The servants had led us to a long oak table graced by a pair of large silver candelabras in the grand dining room. Three chefs stood nearby, alongside a banquet line of culinary treats. Hopefully, the non-poisonous variety. "Did everyone bring their appetites this morning?"

Our host appeared well rested. An old man in his late sixties when he discovered an elixir that made him immortal, his seven hundred and fiftieth birthday was just around the corner. In past encounters, he often displayed more energy than those half his age. That morning, he seemed slightly younger, as the age spots from the previous night had disappeared and the lines around his eyes and upon his forehead were not as deeply etched. His full head of white hair was pulled back in a ponytail, and his attire of a beige sweater and dark slacks made him look more like the dashing lord of this huge estate.

"Smells like kolbalz," said Alistair, the first in line. "If it is, then this will be a real treat."

Immortal Tyranny

"It is," Krontos confirmed. "Have as much as you like, since a big breakfast and lunch will prepare you for your trip this afternoon. And, the weather is perfect!"

As if on cue, the sound of an electric motor high above our heads drew everyone's attention.

"Holy shit," whispered Cedric. "Now that's truly something you don't see every day."

An immense retractable glass ceiling slid open, and the songs of birds filled the air beyond the opening. The castle that had once seemed nothing more than a brooding place for an evil, ink-eyed ogre continued its transformation in my mind to a veritable palace.

Beatrice and Amy gasped in unison as small flocks of birds flew inside and soared near the castle's heights from seemingly nowhere. Colorful birds, I should add. Many resembled blue jays and cardinals, though impossible to define from where we were gathered below.

"Were you expecting an imposing abode run by a vampire like Dracul, Judas?" Krontos laughed. Most of us had taken something to eat from the banquet line and stood as if unsure what to do next. He motioned for everyone to take a seat with him at the table. "You shouldn't be quick to judge those you don't fully understand. I am not like Dracul, but I did love him as a son. I am not bitter against you for what you did to him, as it was simply his time to go. I judge you not for it, nor do I hold the hostility you arrived here with last night against you and your companions. Live and let live. That is the law of the world... of the very universe. Unlike many, I see violence as an answer *only* when it is absolutely necessary."

No one responded to Krontos' expository moment, although I felt certain Roderick shared my silent question.

What in the hell do you want from us?

"I worried you might not ask," said Krontos, obviously privy to my thoughts, and drawing curious looks from everyone but Roderick. "You have the Dragon Coin, which technically was once mine, but more so belongs to you since you've now owned it twice. I am content to let you keep it permanently."

"Oh? How generous, to allow me to keep what's rightfully mine in the first place!"

"Ahh, Judas…. Unwilling to give someone like me a second chance?" he chuckled. "Very well, as I understand. But I truly don't want your coin. Long ago, it served me well… and would serve me just as well again. But, as you have also learned these past two thousand years, good is always better than evil. It's so much *stronger* because of the purity, and will serve me especially well in my efforts to save the world from itself."

"What in the hell are you talking about?" asked Roderick.

Krontos eyed him compassionately, as if he had been reduced to a simpleton overnight.

"I want the coin of the Jews who suffered in Stutthof and Auschwitz," he said. "And, I want you to find it for me, Judas. Its call is known to you better than anyone else."

"Are you telling me that you didn't arrange for our CIA contact and the dealer handling the auction to disappear?" I asked.

"What… to kill them?"

"Yes."

"It wouldn't have been a bad idea, I must admit," he said, pouring a glass of mimosa for himself from a carafe on the table. "But someone else beat me to it."

"And you don't know who it is?" Roderick's contempt and suspicion came shining through.

Immortal Tyranny

"No.... and that's a problem," Krontos replied, gently. "You all understand dimensions and time to some degree, maybe just well enough to be dangerous. Yet, another understands it better than all of you combined. This individual has the coin. Get it back for me, and I will lavish on you gifts far beyond your current wealth. I will also give your lives back, without interference from me ever again."

"And, let's say we can't track down this coin you seek—what then?" I asked. "Will you let us go, even so?"

He eyed me thoughtfully before answering, allowing a slight smile to tug at the corners of his mouth.

"No. You will be my prisoners forevermore," he said, evenly. "So, find it and live."

Talk about a mood crusher. A hush settled upon the table, and my wife sent me a worried look. She subtly shook her head, alerting me that her misgivings about everything were alive and well. The dulled light in her usually bright green eyes revealed her defeated heart. I was beginning to lose her.

"None of us know where to begin, Krontos," I said. "Surely you have some idea of where to begin our search?"

"Unfortunately, I don't have much to give you. I'll gladly share the scant information I have, since this mysterious person showed up in Berlin and disappeared without leaving anything beyond a vapor trail. The rest will be up to you and your instincts. Instincts that have aided your success in finding twenty-five of your thirty blood coins," he said, still smiling. "But, I must warn you, my friend. If you try to escape back to America, the consequences will be severe, and without mercy."

Roderick bristled next to me, and I shared the same aversion to being manipulated. But, without a clear plan in place, this was not the time to protest. Both of us nodded in response, saying nothing.

Immortal Tyranny

Despite the solemn mood among us—other than Krontos, of course—we fed our hunger with mostly Hungarian cuisine. After finishing, we had several hours to roam the castle and grounds before lunch would be served. Krontos advised that I'd be given the keys to our ride from last night, with the initial stop being Auschwitz once more.

"Perhaps you can follow the coin's energy trail better with your loved ones' fate on the line," said Krontos, before taking his leave from us. "In the meantime, you are free to utilize the library upstairs for additional research. Many of the works I've collected over the years deal with subjects that would interest you and Roderick. It will be up to you to utilize all you can before it's time to leave."

Having learned the day's agenda, I spent the first few hours with Beatrice, trying to allay her fears that none of us would survive this latest adventure with our host. She seemed much more terrified of Krontos after meeting him in person, and I found myself leaning more toward her intuitions about him than my own. Especially, in light of how different he seemed from when Roderick and I dealt with him in centuries past.

"No leopard changes its spots beyond the surface," she told me, when I sought to sell the positive aspects of her and Amy staying behind while the guys in our group went looking for the mysterious coin thief. "There is something about him that is worse than what you shared about Viktor Kaslow."

At the time, I didn't agree. But knowing a rebuttal would do little to change her thoughts and feelings, I smiled and confidently assured her that I'd get things sorted out to her liking before all was said and done. She smiled weakly, trying to warm up to my assurances. Afterward, we said little, but explored the first two floors of the revitalized home of our absent host, hand in hand. If things did go badly, we at least had this time together to reflect upon.

Immortal Tyranny

It was nearing noon when we arrived at the library, and I openly wondered then what became of our three Budva escorts from the night before. For all we knew, Krontos had zapped them from our reality, and perhaps the reason why we were being given their smartly outfitted Mercedes for our trip north.

Meanwhile, Roderick had his nose buried in ancient German texts, while Cedric reviewed a large English translation of the works of Guido Von List, noted for being the famous mystic who inspired the Nazis' use of rune symbols and other aspects of German occultism. As for my son and his gal, they were huddled around a computer playing the latest version of Grand Theft Auto.

"I don't believe this shit!" I hissed to Beatrice when we came up behind them. "Everyone else seems to be taking this seriously, while these two—"

"Stop, William!" Beatrice squeezed my fingers and pulled me back from berating the pair, presently caught up in their private revelry. Both wore soundproof headsets and were unaware a very angry 'Dad' stood behind them. "Let them be. This is how your son as a young man blows off stress. You'll see. When you need him to be on point, he'll come through for you. And, surely, there will be something useful he can draw upon from the decades he spent as a decorated academic."

She had a point… well, sort of. But I needed to step away from the nonsense and clear my head. Perhaps wisely, my wife encouraged me to finish our tour of the upstairs areas without her. Since she and Amy would likely have time to look later, she wanted a moment with Alistair before he set out on Krontos' assigned quest with me in a couple of hours. Lunch was supposed to be served around one o'clock, and I told her I'd come back for her. We shared a short, passionate kiss before I set out on my own.

Immortal Tyranny

I hadn't thought about the pair of coins in Krontos' possession since leaving Germany, and hardly anything about his Silver Trinity of Death. However, once I left the second floor and took the long flight of marble stairs to the third floor, a familiar tingling commenced. Only, it was stronger than what I was used to experiencing. Abrupt and very odd. Normally, the sensation begins to hit me when I'm within fifty miles of a blood coin.

The coins... they're near!

The castle had five floors, and the rumor had always been that Krontos' bedchamber was on the fourth floor—one floor below torture chambers of legend, though nothing had ever been verified to Roderick's and my knowledge.

But what lay hidden behind the doors on the third floor, I wondered?

The floor's condition wasn't near as lavish as the rest of the castle we visited thus far. With Krontos' access to unlimited funds, both as an ancient immortal and moving through dimensions to confiscate whatever appealed to him, there likely was another reason for the neglect. This wasn't a floor to be shown off to guests, and it seemed unlikely anyone slept in the half dozen rooms to either side of the gallery overlooking the grand foyer.

Fearful Krontos might suddenly interrupt this unforeseen opportunity to locate my coins, I quieted my breathing and focused my spirit on finding the room. Drawn stronger to the right wing as opposed to the left, I crept along the dusty carpet runner. It seemed almost too obvious that the door pulling me was the middle one, where the carpet's embroidered imagery was slightly less defined due to heavier foot traffic. But, the tingling along my left arm to the point of pain was unmistakable.

Immortal Tyranny

Getting inside the room could be a problem. The other areas we had explored featured areas open for viewing. All doors on this floor were closed, and presumably locked. Tall and heavy, the oak door didn't give at first, despite the latch clicking open. I almost walked away from what could be a bigger problem than it was worth. But I couldn't leave without giving it one good shove.

The door groaned tiredly as it opened. I stepped into a room immersed in darkness. No windows. Two large cobalt halos glowed within the pitch-black environment. The same color as my coins, the size of each was a hundred times too big. It meant something else caused them to glow like this, harkening back to my experience with Genghis Khan's mantle of death.

"There are pictures of those symbols in the book I was reading."

I whirled around in the darkness, pulling out my cell phone to use as a flashlight. Cedric beat me to the punch, shining his Galaxy in my face.

"This is an incredible achievement," he said.

"We can't see much of anything in here," I said, knowing he couldn't see the glow... or could he? Things had changed for the former Agent Tomlinson since his Bolivian experience.

"I'm not talking about what's in here, man. It's awesome that I snuck up on you without you having any idea I've been watching you." He laughed.

"Well, enjoy it while you can, my friend. It'll likely never happen again, I assure you!"

Footsteps from several more people approached, followed by another running to catch up.

"William? Cedric?" Roderick called from outside the door. The rest of our gang was with him

"We're in here, man!" Cedric pointed his cell phone light at the doorway.

Roderick's lanky figure stepped inside followed by Beatrice's wisps of strawberry blonde hair caught in the light's glow. A much smaller figure swept into the room behind them and turned on an overhead light as Amy and Alistair stepped inside.

"Wow," said Roderick, in a hushed, almost reverent tone followed by similar responses from everyone else.

In an instant, a row of crystal chandeliers cast shimmering light upon rows of artifacts. Artifacts from many eras of history. The most obvious were from Constantine, the Inquisition, and Nazi Germany. The bluish objects glowing hotly in the darkness remained, and flanked a swastika banner hanging from a large wooden podium.

"The full 'sun cross' on one side and the broken version on the other. How fitting for a man wanting to make sure he has everything covered," Roderick whispered to me, shortly before Krontos approached. Our host looked both annoyed and amused, and I had a good idea what events corresponded to his bipolar expression. "I wish you luck in getting out of this one without a tongue lashing."

Roderick chuckled as he stepped aside. Beatrice moved closer, as if to protect me. I couldn't help but smile.

"Well, Judas, if nothing else, I see your ability to track energy trails is as strong as ever. That's very good, since you'll need that gift to find my coin," he said, moving toward the twin steel stands supporting the slightly different sun crosses. He lovingly stroked the banner as if it belonged to a Christian saint. "Would you all like to hear a little story about Adolf Hitler?"

Not really. After all, we had recently visited two terrible sites created by the man's depravity, and were about to revisit Auschwitz.

Immortal Tyranny

"Bear with me anyway," said Krontos, a slight reddish glow tinting his irises, the wrath apparently harder to subdue. I guess I wasn't supposed to find this sacred place of his. "Adolf Hitler was referred to me by a friend who discovered this charismatic lad in his early days. Though merely a casual acquaintance at first, I soon saw what he could be and began to groom him for the role he was perfect for. It has always been a proud moment to know I influenced the rise and fall of the Third Reich."

"You really were friends with Hitler?"

Heat embraced my face and crept down my shoulders and back. I deeply resented the fact Krontos had aligned himself with such a devil, but to call Hitler a friend? It took a supreme effort not to lash out at him.

"Why, of course," he said, smiling slyly. "But, you and others misjudge my friendship with him. History only sees the bad of Hitler, and largely because his reign was cut short. Very few great leaders of the world would be seen as benevolent, if their reign ended prematurely and before a purge of those who stood in the way of the new order of things was successful. The Nazis were no more evil, as you are apt to think, Judas, than Genghis Khan, Alexander the Great, or Julius Caesar, to name a few. Hitler's reign was incomplete. And, know this, as your anger begins to boil against me, old friend, your ancestors once sought to purge what they considered impure nations from the land they invaded. The 'Land of Canaan' was no more ordained by Almighty God to be handed to the Israelites than Europe to the Germans. Were the Canaanites allowed to coexist with the new invaders flooding into their homeland? Hmmmm? Or, even where you reside now, how many ethnic Native Americans remain, after nearly four hundred years of slaughter and discrimination, and moments like Andrew Jackson's Trail of Tears forced upon the proud Cherokee?"

Hard to refute what happened in America after the first white settlers arrived along the eastern seaboard. If not for the rise of profitable gambling facilities, the last of America's native peoples could be extinct by the end of the twenty-first century. More inconvenient was the dig against my Jewish brethren. As anyone familiar with Hebrew history, or the Torah and Old Testament, will tell you, the Gentile peoples living in the 'Promised Land' were in fact purged by my ancestors. Under the auspices of Jehovah, no less. Was it genocide on a much smaller scale? Perhaps… but many of the Canaanites were eventually absorbed into Hebrew society. That alone refuted Krontos' skewed view.

Regardless, nothing could ever support the actions of the Nazis, whose motives were more likely rooted in removing the economic status of those who controlled the wealth of Europe in the early twentieth century. What better way to do it than to feed a propaganda campaign designed to dehumanize Jewish people? Turn them into animals and one can steal their possessions. Shamefully, this concept has long been with us as a race. Examples in my new homeland, America, include Salem, during the witch trials, and the aforementioned Trail of Tears, the removal of 'savages' from white civilization.

"So you see, Judas. Pushing one nation aside to make room for another has been a hallmark of mankind for thousands of years," continued Krontos, ignoring my indignation to speak. "It certainly should give pause to those humanists who believe the human race is evolving, eh?"

"Maybe the human race hasn't evolved to where we should be by now," I conceded. "However, the level of cruelty demonstrated by Nazi Germany was unprecedented. Not even your protégé, Vlad Tepes, could top the barbaric and systematic removal of one's enemies like Hitler and his cohorts set out to do. And, if the Germans had won the war, by now

Immortal Tyranny

their unsustainable philosophy would have run its course and we would be fighting through an unfathomable anarchy—the likes the world has never seen."

Alistair offered a proud nod, and I could almost feel Roderick's pleasure at a response to shut down the rhetoric. But this was Krontos' turf, and to humiliate him was dangerous.

"It is best to please the host, indeed," he said, smiling smugly as he announced his response to my thoughts before the group. Most were getting used to it by now, although Amy and Beatrice exchanged curious glances until they saw the acknowledgement on my face. "We should break for lunch and send the boys on their way. Shall we?"

He motioned politely for our ladies to go first and the rest to follow. As he shut the lights behind us, I took one last glance at the pair of sun circles glowing in the sudden darkness. From a distance, the glistening blue symbols of the Third Reich reminded me of my coins, still hidden somewhere in the castle. Could they somehow be responsible for the familiar light?

It became the only thing I could think about, until it was time to leave for Auschwitz.

Chapter Fifteen

I was reluctant to release Beatrice from the tight embrace we shared. Cultivating a mutual fear of what lay ahead, it felt wrong to leave her behind with Krontos. As the guys and I headed north, my mind was repeatedly drawn to her and the Nazi sun crosses we had seen upstairs in the castle. Had Krontos defiled my blood coins to where they now performed a diabolical function far beyond their original accursed status? After all, what else could cause their steel casings to glow with a cobalt sheen?

"A better question is why does Krontos wish to deal with a coin that has only brought blessings to the Jewish family carrying it for so many years?" said Roderick, picking up on my silent musings. For the trip north, Roderick usurped the driving privileges, and I joined him up front. Alistair and Cedric sat behind us. "With his obvious affections for Hitler and the Nazis' agenda, you would think he would fear retribution from The Almighty."

I had considered the same thing, and wondered if it would similarly curse the murdering thief who took it from Franz Reifenstahl. But after Krontos provided us with no more details surrounding the murders than we already gathered on our own, finding out who killed the dealer and took the coin seemed virtually impossible. Without a miracle, we would be searching for the proverbial needle in a haystack.

Immortal Tyranny

"Are you pilfering Pops' head again?" Alistair quipped, drawing a chuckle from Cedric. "Because if you are, it would be polite to let those of us in the backseat know what silent question prompted your response."

Roderick and I exchanged amused glances and smirks.

"All right, Ali. I was thinking about something you guys probably missed detecting inside Krontos' 'tyrant relics' room," I said. "Something unusual."

"What? That his Nazi crosses were glowing blue?"

Damn. Cedric saw that shit?

"Yeah, it's one way to describe them," I said, feeling sorry for my kid, who looked irritated being excluded again. "To be honest, I'm not sure what to think of the room's contents."

"Well, it seems fitting that a crazy old immortal would be the asshole to influence the worst genocidal campaign in history—even if it wasn't his original intent to kill every Jew in Europe," said Alistair, deflecting the conversation away from what his eyes couldn't discern.

"The hell you say, son." My inner temperature began to rise as my pity evaporated. "It was always Krontos' intent to kill each and every Jew residing in Europe. *Always*. He could've stopped it, too, and did not. He hates—"

"Those of Hebrew descent?" interrupted Roderick. "Absolutely, which is why I'm reminding you to *never* trust him. Krontos is asking us to retrieve one of the few noble objects to emerge from the war, and you know his intent will never benefit the good of mankind. It's obviously the centerpiece of his latest master plan. I'm surprised, though, that you didn't hear the louder call of two coins this time. Maybe carrying the Dragon Coin on your person muted the others' response, or hindered your ability to hear either one's call."

"I heard at least one of my other coins call to me this morning," I confessed. "At least one is in the castle, and I believe they both are. Likely, they're somewhere near the circle crosses. Otherwise, what else could cause these Nazi occult symbols to glow like that? Once Krontos entered the room, the sensation of ownership ceased, but those damned crosses continued to glow. Maybe Krontos has created something that mimics the glow of my blood coins."

"Sounds like this old buddy of yours is having a ball messing with your head," said Cedric. "Hell, man, it's Halloween. Maybe none of the shit we saw in the castle is real. Of course, if that's true, then we are four of the sorriest dumbasses to ever live, pursuing a wild goose chase while Beatrice and Amy are at this monster's mercy."

"Krontos has never been a friend," I said. Sourness seized my stomach. "This feels more and more like a mistake. Rod, what if Cedric's right?"

Roderick hesitated before responding, perhaps still sorting through Cedric's observation.

"Anything is possible," he said, for the moment maintaining our present course. It would be roughly an hour's journey to the castle, should we abort our trip to Poland and immediately return. "But before we throw caution to the wind and head back to face an angry and potentially violent menace, we need to consider everything very seriously. We can't afford to take Krontos' latest threats lightly. I doubt we'd get the same mercy we received last night for disobeying his edict to stay put in America. He seemed almost hostile this afternoon in his directive to not return to Hungary without a winning lead to tracking down the coin's location.

"Yeah, he was a complete asshole," Cedric agreed.

"Who cares if Krontos was a jerk? Pops, maybe you should've said something about your misgivings to him before we left," said Alistair, accusingly. His ruddy complexion was turning ashen. "Better yet, you could've listened to Mom and

Immortal Tyranny

headed back to Berlin yesterday from Auschwitz, instead of pressing forward into Hungary. I think we made a big mistake in coming."

His handsome brown eyes that had always encouraged comparisons to Sean Connery, and made me think of my older brother Joseph, misted without their usual gleam. His shoulders heaved, but then he caught himself. An admirable effort to keep the churning emotional deluge at bay.

"I know you're worried about Amy and your mom," I told him, mindful to sound compassionate, and holding back my indignation at being chastised like a damned fool. "I'm worried too, Ali. But Krontos doesn't make idle threats. We had no choice other than to cooperate with his whims."

"Krontos strikes me as a solution kind of guy," Cedric interjected. "As in *Final Solution*. Since we won't reach Auschwitz until after the place closes, maybe we've been set up for failure. And, that's taking in consideration what I heard him mention about easier detection of residual energy at night. Just sayin'."

Admittedly, things looked increasingly grim. Not to mention, Krontos didn't give us much to go on from the outset, despite earlier assurances to the contrary. In addition to the bullshit about detecting extinct energy trails at night, only our accommodations in Berlin were discussed. Along with a promise for more information to be delivered when we arrived at the hotel picked out by Krontos. The Rocco Forte Hotel.

As for our upcoming Auschwitz visit, Roderick and I were instructed to seek specific 'psychic' connections from the barracks to the Nazis who took possession of the Stutthof-Auschwitz coin. From there, the idea was to somehow track the faint essence of the coin using the same kind of images. Once in Berlin, our instructions were to focus on the final moments of Franz Riefenstahl's earthly existence. Hopefully, we'd catch

Immortal Tyranny

a glimpse of the murdering thief who lifted the coin from Riefenstahl's corpse.

"I agree this all seems like a slipshod assignment," I said. "Tell you what, guys... let me call Beatrice. If the conversation feels out of sorts—regardless of what she says to assure me otherwise—we'll turn around and head back to the castle."

Roderick hesitated at first, but everyone soon supported the idea. Fortunately, the cell reception was good enough to make the connection, though I could tell from the static between rings that a clear conversation would be difficult.

"Hey, hon'." Beatrice answered, her tone worried. "Are you all right?" I pictured Krontos standing nearby, listening while watching her reaction.

"Yes, we're fine. Just wanted to hear your voice, and let you know the weather is holding up. We should reach Auschwitz by eight o'clock, as planned," I said, cheerfully.

"I miss you, too, William. It seems nuts to be visiting Auschwitz at that late hour. I hope Krontos knows what he's talking about. Try not to get arrested for trespassing." She laughed weakly.

I laughed with her, feeling better about her and Amy's immediate welfare. It seemed Krontos wasn't around after all. Still, it wasn't wise to linger, in case he watched her remotely.

"Darling, keep your phone handy," I advised, signaling to my comrades I was about to hang up. "I'll call you as soon as we have some good news."

Keeping my voice cheerful, I moved to close the call. Beatrice sounded more assured... it worked.

"You look pleased," noted Roderick. "Anything we should be concerned about?"

"No. Beatrice sounded upbeat. So did Amy in the background," I said. "They're fine for now."

Immortal Tyranny

"I heard you tell Mom that you'll check in with her later tonight. When you do, I'd like to visit with Amy for just a moment," said Alistair. Krontos had confiscated Amy's phone at lunch, when we agreed to limit the conversations between Beatrice and myself. Two phone calls per day, until we returned to the castle.

"We'll see, son. If Krontos isn't hovering like a hawk, maybe you and Amy can visit for a minute." Pained by the longing in his face, it was the same for me in regard to Beatrice. I loathed the hypocrisy I felt for my privilege to speak with my wife. "But, the sooner we complete our task, the sooner we can get back to them."

For the next several hours we continued our trek, stopping for supper in Nowy Sacz, roughly two hours from Auschwitz. By the time we finished our meal, a heavy snowstorm that started in the afternoon made the going slow and arduous. It became apparent we wouldn't fulfill our assignment from Krontos that night.

"Looks like we will need to stop somewhere, and pick this up again in the morning," I said, after Roderick translated a local radio weather report. The snow was supposed to cease around midnight, but the treacherous driving conditions wouldn't improve until mid-morning the next day. "Either that, or find a local peasant pulling a sled."

"We should try to reach Krakow," Roderick suggested, ignoring my joke. "One of us will have the unenviable task of contacting Krontos with the news our arrival at Auschwitz and Berlin will be delayed. Hopefully, we can visit the camp in the morning when it opens, and be on our way to Germany by tomorrow afternoon."

"I bet that'll be fun," jested Cedric, while he watched the snow mercilessly pelt the Mercedes as Roderick fought to keep it on the road. "Didn't you say the other night that Krontos' temper was like a scorpion backed into a corner? Right? I know one of y'all said it."

"Pops did." Alistair seemed subdued, as if the snow had derailed much more than our Auschwitz assignment.

"I should be the one to call him, Rod," I said, offering a hopeful smile to my kid, who waved me off. "I doubt he'll be happy about it, but he needs to frigging remember two of us are immortal, and two are not. If the youngsters catch their death of cold, all of us will be up shit's creek trying to make this crazy assignment work."

Roderick agreed.

"He shouldn't get too upset," added Cedric, snickering. "If he does, I'd ask him how he expects us to find anything in this weather. In fact, I'd bet he never expected us to find anything out here anyway. With all the agency tricks I've taught you, Willie Boy, you should see right through his shit screen."

"What the hell do you mean?" I asked, warily. My former CIA field supervisor wasn't always the epitome of nobility during my days working for him. However, more often than not his instincts and observations were spot on. "What shit screen?"

"The one that says he never expects us to find jack at Auschwitz," said Cedric. "I can't see what you and Roderick see or sense. But I felt something at Auschwitz. A second visit ain't gonna help anything. Nothing will be any clearer, man. My gut tells me Krontos knows it, too."

"Then, why did he send us out here?" asked Alistair, worriedly.

Great. This was all we needed. More frigging drama... I began to envision strangling Cedric if he didn't shut the hell up.

"Well, even though your dad is super pissed at me for sharing my honest thoughts, and Roderick might be, too, I bet

Krontos is laughing at us. This asshole—and he's probably listening in right now—doesn't expect us to find anything. So, why did he send us back to Auschwitz? That answer I don't know for sure yet. But do y'all recall what he taunted us with this morning? He said whoever took the coin in Berlin had a superior understanding of dimensions and how to move through them—much better than all of us combined. If that's the case, what idiot worth any salt would assign a group of 'dimensional amateurs', like us, to do a job only a pro could handle?"

I wanted to hit him. Really I did. But, I also felt like a bigger asshole than the one he taunted. Cedric was right, and the answer about why this aura-following adventure had felt doomed from the beginning was staring us straight in the face.

"Well, then what do we do now?" asked Roderick, glancing repeatedly in the rearview mirror, as if expecting Krontos to suddenly appear behind him. "Do we continue to Krakow, since it's getting late?"

"What? So we can hole up in a hostel and discuss this silliness further?" Cedric sounded amazed and disgusted. This had to be a sweet moment for him, on some level.

"Touche, Boss," I said. "I don't know the right answer either. Maybe no one does."

I reached for my phone. None of the guys tried to stop me from dialing Beatrice again. I didn't know what to expect, but began to worry when the fourth ring arrived. Just before getting routed to a Polish cellular network recording, my wife answered.

At first I couldn't hear her, and assumed we had a compromised call connection. Prepared to hang up and try again, I heard screaming. Amy screaming.

"William?! He's gone *mad!*" cried Beatrice. "I can't hear what you're saying, William! If you hear me, *please* come back! Don't leave us here! *Don't—*"

"*Beatrice!*"

The line was dead. Worse, my ensuing calls to her phone were unsuccessful.

The decision what to do next had been made. Roderick spun the SUV around, sliding dangerously in the snow near a guardrail, and headed south—praying we'd get back to the castle before the unthinkable happened.

Immortal Tyranny

Chapter Sixteen

I should have expected betrayal. Especially, given my very personal past with Krontos. I doubt anyone would blame me for the fantasy of tearing the little bastard limb from limb. I could justifiably subject him to the same tortures he delivered to Roderick and me long ago as a Cardinal Inquisitor. Dracul may have been the one administering most of our excruciating torments, but the Hungarian monster was never far removed from the events, like a closet pervert.

But for the moment, none of that mattered. All I could think of was reaching my beloved Beatrice and Amy before something horrible happened to either one, or both. My wife's panic repeated in my mind as I urged Roderick to drive faster, egged on by the mental echoes from Amy's terrified screams.

"You're going to have to let me drive without distraction, William. You'll get us killed if you don't!" he warned, after nearly taking the Mercedes over a steep embankment. Cedric and Alistair clung to seatbelts and door restraints with white-knuckled tenacity. "We can only go so fast!"

"Think about the mortals in the backseat, Pops—I'm freaking out just as badly as you about Mom and Amy! Don't get us killed trying to reach the castle at breakneck speed!"

Alistair's complexion had taken on a green tint. One more hairpin turn taken at my suggested ninety-kilometer clip would surely expose the front seat to a shower of vomit, if we didn't flip over a guardrail first.

"Okay," I said, drawing a deep breath and holding it for a moment before slowly exhaling. It wasn't fair for me to suddenly behave like I was the only one in the vehicle with something precious to lose. "Drive safely, then… but work the road to the best of your ability, Rod. You know all too well what Krontos is capable of—despite his cheerful façade the past two days."

"Yes, I do," Roderick agreed. "I still have scars from when he burned my flesh away in Madrid. Remember? I showed you them when we caught up with each other in Athens, 1494. It was nearly ten years after you disappeared, when Dracul killed you."

"How could I forget?" I said softly, my heightened eagerness subdued by the memory. "I woke up in Cairo, in a ghetto, and was soon arrested for stealing a small loaf of bread."

It wasn't our first Inquisition imprisonment together, but it was the first time I succumbed to the physical tortures involved. Serious wounds to vital organs bled faster than my body could heal. Nearly two hundred years since my last death and immediate reincarnation, I had forgotten the raging hunger that accompanies these rebirths. Four years fighting for my life in another dingy dungeon followed, under the watchful eyes of Egyptian taskmasters. By the time my joyful reunion with Roderick took place, nine years had passed since we last spoke. Fearing his death at the hands of the Inquisition, my constant worry was that I'd be forced to walk the earth alone.

"I didn't bring this up to reopen old wounds," he said, eyeing me compassionately. "I just wanted you to never forget that I *know* what kind of fiend we are up against."

"What was it like to face this asshole back then? Did he make you feel naked on the inside, and violated when he invaded your private thoughts?" Cedric frowned as if he never intended to share anything he personally experienced with Krontos.

Roderick shook his head and I barely acknowledged Cedric's questions, as well. But when Alistair echoed Cedric's curiosity, there wasn't a way to cleanly avoid an explanation.

"He was more of an annoyance than anything else," said Roderick, glancing warily at me. "Always there, lurking. I could feel him... boiling over with rage and hate I assumed at the time was merely ignorant jealousy of my youth. Bitter for the years it took him to find the right elixir to grant him eternal life, Krontos loathed the fact he would be a crotchety old man for all eternity, while people like Judas and me would not. But, did I fear his sorcerer skills at the time? No. And, I never experienced what you say you dealt with, Cedric. Maybe this is something new. Like the dimension manipulation talent he has since been endowed with. He didn't possess that ability back then."

"I never experienced anything like what you described either, Cedric," I said. "But the cleverness he employed to track us down and imprison us—once in the fourteenth century and twice in the fifteenth—speaks to the same compulsion to invade a person's privacy. Whether that means a hostile takeover of one's life or mind, the violation is the same."

"That's a lot to assume, Pops," commented Alistair, chuckling. "You can't equate the two behaviors so simply. What seems more accurate is to say the two invasive habits are related to Krontos' psychopathic curiosity."

"What in the hell are you talking about, Ali?" Cedric straightened in his seat to better regard my boy and his smugness—the last vestige of the once-grandfatherly history professor at Georgetown. "You're becoming more and more like your old man every day."

"Krontos is nothing more than a control freak," said Alistair, smiling playfully. "A control freak with serious issues."

"*Murderous* issues," I corrected him, beginning to worry about Alistair's steady drift from the balanced pragmatist he once was. "Make that a murderous psychopath with an opportunistic flair."

"*What?!* See what I'm talking about, you two? Don't feed us more bullshit, Judas!" Cedric's brow furrowed deeply as he shook his head disgustedly.

"It's not bullshit, Cedric. If you stop and think about it, Krontos is not so different from the host of miscreants that joined the Nazi movement. Everyone from Himmler to Mengele, and so many who later returned to peaceful lives after World War II, were drawn to the opportunity to act out their psychopathic compulsions—largely because there were no consequences for having such designs," I explained. "Mengele and Klaus Barbie made a great impression on their South American neighbors, and no one who knew them in their later years could believe they were the vicious monsters who tortured and murdered thousands during the war."

"Do you think Krontos will act like these war criminals to Mom and Amy?"

Alistair's worry deepened. I suddenly wished I had just agreed with him and avoided my mini-lecture on Krontos' Nazi affiliations and bent toward similar wickedness.

"Not before we get there," I sought to assure him. "I refuse to believe The Almighty will allow us to fail. But you have seen enough of the man's wiles since we left Abingdon to know we must come up with an effective plan. Otherwise, he will have us all in chains if we can't surprise him."

As if on cue, a powerful gust of wind swept across the highway and nearly shoved us into oncoming traffic.

Immortal Tyranny

"Better start working on a plan right now," Roderick advised when he regained control of the Mercedes. His eyes were swirling hot pools of blue and gold, like a kaleidoscope on fire. "I can get us there in about five hours, but we need the details ironed out before we reach the castle grounds first."

* * * * *

The plan we came up with was a good one. Some aspects were exceptional, I thought. But the trouble with plotting against a fiend with access to awareness beyond normal comprehension is the likelihood that whatever we came up with, Krontos would remain a step ahead. Of course, if we had simply acknowledged that fact, then why even bother? A complex attack would be just as ineffective as a bull rush to storm the castle gates.

The first idea was Roderick's, and with better access to GPS maps than either of us expected, we altered our route just enough to not retrace our path back to the Mátra Mountains. Instead, we returned to the outskirts of Budapest and headed east to the mountains—similar to the route taken by Krontos' hoodlums the night before.

But we should've known any attempt to invade the ancient sorcerer's stomping grounds undetected would fail. Subtle at first, Roderick's and my wariness picked up something predatory as we neared the southern border of Slovakia.

"You feel it?" I asked him, quietly, when he took his eyes off the road to peer out the passenger windows.

"It started near Lučenec, and has steadily grown stronger," he replied. "Maybe it will fade... maybe it isn't him."

"Who?" Alistair poked his head between the front seats. "Are you talking about Krontos?"

"Yes," I confessed. "But it's nothing to be concerned about yet."

"There you go again... when you should realize the James Bond clandestine approach won't work," said Cedric, his head next to Alistair's. "Not on us."

Roderick smirked and shook his head, glancing at me with a wan smile.

"Okay." I released a low sigh, hoping it would buy me a moment to think of a diversion to discuss anything other than the brooding presence of a paranoid immortal watching from some unseen vantage point. But there was nothing. Just the truth of what I felt—what Roderick, and probably Cedric and Alistair, felt, too. "He knows we're coming."

"See, Pops? That's *exactly* what I warned you about in Poland, when you wouldn't let me try to call Mom and Amy!" said Alistair, angrily. "If nothing else, I could've made sure they were all right!"

"Or, ensured their demise," said Roderick, butting in before I could offer the same rebuke. His response lacked the ire that surely would've come with mine. "Especially with Krontos on the move, spiritually, when he is at his most unpredictable. Likely, he is listening to us now. It would be in everyone's best interest to remain calm, follow the plan we laid out three hours ago, and let me drive."

"Rod's right, Ali," I said, as the pair sat back in their seats, while releasing their own frustrated sighs. "This is a time for faith in doing the smartest things, and not giving in to thoughts of panic. We *will* save Beatrice and Amy—trust me, if you can't trust anything else."

Yeah, that sounded flimsy to me, too. As we crossed into Hungary, the feeling of impending doom suddenly intensified. Like an inquisitive fly that had drifted too close to a black widow's nest. Obviously, we couldn't turn around and look for a haven back in Slovakia. Regardless of what we'd soon face, time was not on our side, and Alistair's worry about our cherished women would be well founded if we took too long to reach the castle.

"I don't know about you two, but I definitely don't like the way this feels," said Cedric. "Whatever you guys felt twenty minutes ago has got to be worse now."

"It's stronger," I told him, peering at him and my boy in the back seat. Both were grimacing as if we had just run over a small army of skunks. "Try to clear your minds, and don't linger long on any one thought. I'll explain why this works later on. For now, just trust me."

Roderick smiled for a moment, in what I supposed was some level of admiration for my advice. Then his expression turned somber, and worsened once we veered onto the highway that would take us to Krontos' castle in the mountains.

I believe all of us were afraid to say anything else. Other than making a pit stop to refuel and grab a bite to eat, we were focused on reaching our destination as quickly as possible. And, our plan? The idea was to get as close as possible to the castle without encouraging a face to face confrontation with Krontos' men—nearly two dozen by Cedric and Roderick's estimation. Since we'd likely need the car to make a getaway when we retrieved our precious cargo, I suggested cutting the engine and headlights once we crossed a slight incline in the road, roughly a hundred meters from the castle grounds to avoid detection. The optimal hope was to coast down the road until within easy sprinting distance of the gates, and making our final approach on foot.

On foot, and unarmed. Pure insanity—especially if the bad guys carrying the latest weaponry cut us down from hidden vantage points. Foolhardy determination to rescue a pair of damsels in serious distress was the only thing in our favor... or destined to be our doom, depending on how one looked at the situation.

Almost 2:00 a.m. when we reached the incline point, the eerie feeling suddenly dissipated. I assumed Alistair and Cedric would notice and say something about it. But neither one did. Instead, they prepared to exit the Mercedes. The look on Roderick's face told me that he felt the shift... sort of like how the sensation started, back in Poland.

"Everyone clear on what to do?" I asked. Alistair and Cedric nodded in the backseat's dimness while Roderick parked the vehicle between a pair of thick evergreens. Slightly more moonlight than the night before, the car was impossible to hide, unless we wanted to run the risk of it rolling off the mountainside. Unfortunately, our best camouflage came when we coasted in silence. It would have to be enough, given everything we were up against. "Follow my lead and keep up."

Moving through snow past our ankles, I led the way to the gates with Cedric right behind me. I could hear Roderick prodding Alistair to stay ahead of him, and expected gunfire in response. But there was nothing... and seemingly no one outside, as I scanned the moonlit landscape around us.

The castle turrets came into view, where the rooftops glowed eerily. But to my surprise, the place was dark.

"What in the hell?" whispered Roderick, in disbelief. Cedric and Alistair murmured similarly.

So lonely in appearance, the place looked deserted. Not a damned light or sign of life anywhere.

"This can't be happening," murmured Alistair, while all of us moved in a protective circle.

Sitting ducks for a sniper, the glowering presence of something else drew our attention. From inside the castle? Hard to say. An unfamiliar presence, it carried a scent I recognized.

"The place looks like it's falling apart, man." Cedric pointed to the castle's main entrance, where large pieces of brick and mortar had fallen from the balcony above it, smashing a gas lantern near the front steps. "Is this Krontos' doing, or someone else?"

"Hard to say. I think we should have a look inside," I said. "Your thoughts, Rod?"

"I think Krontos is still here... somewhere. So, yes, we should take a look," he concurred. "Just be aware that what we see right now might not be part of our reality. It could be another dimensional shift... but why?"

"Maybe we pissed him off a lot worse than we thought," said Alistair, running to the entrance after taking one last precautionary look toward the roof and windows. "I've got to go find Amy, and Pops, you need to look for Mom!"

"Wait, Ali—don't go in there yet!"

But it was too late. The front door ajar, he easily pushed it open and stepped inside. Cedric followed, using the penlight on his phone to illuminate the foyer's darkness while my boy searched for a light switch... then a floor lamp... and finally settling on a torch lying near the foot of the grand staircase. Cedric was helping him light the damned thing with a cigarette lighter when Roderick and I stepped inside the entrance.

"It's freezing in here, Pops, and the furniture is broken. And...." Alistair held the torch in front of him as he whirled around. Everywhere the light touched revealed a dank and dirty environment. "Everyone's *gone!* Where in the hell did they go?!"

"Ali," I said, gently, moving to restrain him from running up the stairs. "It's not what it seems. This isn't the *right* reality. Krontos has done something, and we have to figure out—"

"Oh, shut the hell up, Pops!" he said angrily, ripping at my fingers to release the grasp I had on his coat sleeve. Roderick joined me in restraining him when he fought to remove his coat. "Damn it let me go! Fuck Krontos and his schemes! *Amy! Mom!*"

Alistair's voice echoed hollowly throughout the foyer and into the darkened rooms and halls beyond the torch glow's reach. The echoes seemed to take on a life of their own... until I realized it was laughter in a similar pitch to Alistair's voice. Derisive in tone, it approached us from the dimness beyond the stairs.

"Fuck *who?*"

More laughter, and then Krontos appeared before us. Disheveled and snarling, his eyes were completely black. Like an Estonian vampire, he leered at each of us, lingering longest on my son, and sending a surge of angst through my heart.

"Please don't direct your anger at him," I said, pleadingly, angry at myself for not muzzling my kid. "If you must exact punishment for what has happened, then let it be on me. Let them go... along with Amy and Beatrice."

He turned his livid cold gaze to me, regarding me with contempt. But then he smiled, revealing a mouth filled with decay—likely the very same set of teeth he had two hundred years ago. His smile grew brighter, surely in response to my mortified reaction to his presence.

"Hmmm.... You are repulsed, Judas. No?"

"None of this matters. You can do with me as you wish."

He laughed, and if not for his obnoxious presence, I would say merrily. Then the laughter stopped abruptly and he approached where I stood, until his presence became too painful to endure.

"This is your fault, and you shall pay!" he said, menacingly, leaning up against me. "You are responsible for *all* of this! Because of what you did to *him*, I have suffered! Now, you must be punished!"

"I don't understand—"

"You *must* be punished!"

The room seemed to shake with this last condemnation, and it chilled my bones and very soul like nothing I had ever experienced before. I reached out to where Roderick had stood only a moment before, but he was gone. Same for Alistair and Cedric. They had all disappeared!

"You must be punished!" Krontos shrieked. The walls around us were changing, seemingly on fire.

Stuck in this hell, with the diminutive monster getting more agitated by the moment, hope of salvation faded fast. I had no answers.

Only a shared destiny with the devil himself.

Chapter Seventeen

Even without an unfamiliar environment superimposed over the one I was barely familiar with, Krontos had me at a distinct disadvantage. If this meant merely dealing with an immortal with the standard regenerative traits existing in varying degrees within us all, it would be one thing. But trying to anticipate the mischief coming from a master of sorcery on levels that far exceeded any alchemist I had ever known? It would be easier to solve a Rubik's Cube blindfolded.

"You and your brood should have stayed in Poland!" Krontos sneered. "You led him right to us—how much of a fool do you take me for?"

"What in the hell are you talking about? Whom do you mean by *him?*"

Krontos didn't reply with an answer, other than a roar reminiscent of a hyena howling in distress. Much more disturbing than I can describe, it was merely the vocal portion of his response. What followed was worse. *Much* worse.

I had forgotten the source for his superhuman strength came from his mastery of physics, or the displacement of atoms or some shit. But a quick refresher was on the way. Before I could set my defensive stance in anticipation of a medieval form of hand-to-hand combat, he sent a blast of crimson light from his palms opened outward. The quickness alone surprised me, and before I could react I was airborne, on my way to crashing

Immortal Tyranny

against an unforgiving marble wall across the foyer from where our battle embarked.

The blow would've permanently paralyzed or killed a mere mortal. But by the time my fractured body crumpled to the ground, my broken back and lacerated internal organs were seized by the warm tingle of healing. The injuries' searing pain abated as I struggled to my feet.

"Words will get you a helluva lot further with me than violence, Krontos," I said, forcing a smile. All I wanted to do was tear his frigging head off. But that would surely spell the end for my family and friends. Outfoxing this psychopath might be an impossible feat, but I had to try. "I might be able to heal fast and figure out most things quickly…. But unless you tell me the name of this mysterious person, I doubt I'll figure out who it is."

"Oh. So, you think an identity will absolve your guilt?" He laughed, throwing off the robe before moving stealthily toward me, like an albino monkey in his crouched nakedness. Not since a battle with a Pixie during Rome's brief occupation of Great Britain had I dealt with a gonad-swinging elf like this madman. And, perhaps it was the intent. His smile returned, more maniacal than before. "Suppose it would be much more fun to torture your body beyond its regenerative abilities, by beating you senseless and giving scant clues to the riddle, while you also worry about the fate of your loved ones? Such an exercise would be especially rewarding, and harkens back to my favorite Nazi pupils, like Josef Mengele. You've heard of his exploits recently, no doubt, and perhaps you are as big a fan of his deadly efficiency as I am. No?"

"The Angel of Death was one of the most despicable cowards the world has ever known. An evil man who tortured and stole the lives of thousands during his lifetime," I replied, keeping enough distance to prevent the creepy old man from lunging at my legs. "What's there to be proud of? If he were someone you influenced, I'd say you scraped the very bottom of the shithead barrel with that one. Even lower than reanimating the corpse of Vlad Tepes."

"Revived!" Krontos responded, testily. "I revived Dracul, and could do so again if it served my ambitions."

He lunged, grasping in desperation at my legs. I leaped over him, barely escaping his bony fingers that suddenly lengthened with fingernails curled inward. The Gollum-esque illusion was short lived, and he returned to his naturally despicable state.

"You act like you saved his life, and that it was a good thing, " I said, putting more distance between us. "All you did was enhance his wickedness as a mortal and ensure his permanent residence in hell."

We had in effect switched places, and I carefully stepped back toward the stairs. The immense oak doors that marked the castle's entrance stood to my left—the only possible exit to freedom from this soulless villain. But the salvation of those I cherished meant either searching the darkened halls on the main level or taking my chances upstairs. It seemed most unwise to try and scurry past the shape-shifting ogre bearing down on me, leaving upstairs as my only valid option.

"What do you know about permanent residences in hell, Judas?" He quickly cut the distance between us to where his foul breath filled my nostrils. "Do you still believe your God will allow the redemption of your pitiful soul in exchange for your blood money?"

Words on their own should never hurt, since ideas in themselves are not physical things, like rocks, knives, and bullets. But an accusation mirroring my own guilt—the burden I have carried for centuries—took the wind out of me. My legs began to shake, and I feared I might collapse.

"Better to make deals with the various powers that arise in this world!" Krontos crowed when I didn't respond. He puffed out his chest, surely sensing I would soon be at his complete mercy. "But you are too weak for that, Judas! That is how you and I are different, and always will be. If it had been me betraying Jesus, instead of you, I wouldn't have mourned the decision or the consequences. I would've watched his agony and thought little of it—nothing beyond the fact another Jewish Messiah had failed to lead his people—the Jews. Forever vermin and the scourge of this earth! Jews like you and your pathetic, spineless boy, Alistair. He is just like *you!*"

My strength wilted, and my legs and arms felt increasingly heavy. My fading life force matched his approach, and he crept into my personal space. I had to get away from him... somehow... get away, or die. But I couldn't move. Not until I glimpsed something large and dark fluttering above the ornate newel post at the top of the stairs. When I turned to see what it was, it moved away... more like *flew* away.

What in the hell was that?

Krontos' menacing dark gaze followed mine, and the leering smile faded slightly.

He's worried? Something about whatever's up there scares him.... Yes, I see it in his eyes.

The brooding presence above did seem threatening, and yet, also familiar. I had encountered it before—I felt certain of this fact. And, I was just as certain Krontos had little or no experience dealing with anything like it. In all the dimensional journeys he had taken during his extended lifetime, he acted like this was a first encounter, and it threw him out of his comfort zone.

He looked warily toward the top of the stairs, largely unaware I had stepped away from him. Whether it would mean greater danger, or not, I decided to let fate take its course.

Immortal Tyranny

"Do you really believe the demons will spare you?" asked Krontos, after I put a few more stairs between us and neared the second floor. Energy began to return to me, and the faint call of my coins grew stronger. I said nothing in response and picked up my pace. "An old friend will be so delighted to see you!"

Krontos' latest taunt sent a powerful chill across my spine, and I paused to look above. The second floor sat empty... but part of the banister was missing from earlier, and the break looked unnatural. A fallen torch burned on the floor nearby, revealing the railing's exposed layers of gold, wrought iron, and marble—the stratification much cleaner than if something had blasted or burned its way through these layers.

"Go to him, Jew Dog!" Krontos hissed from behind, I pushed away his hands as he reached for my ankles. "Go to him, and after your friend tears you from limb to limb, as he told me earlier he would, I will enjoy prosperity and peace again!"

I stepped onto the floor, moving to the gallery. Several more dark shapes drifted toward me from the dark expanse above the torch.

Sounds like an army of these suckers... what are they?

"Is there ever honor among miscreants like you, Krontos?" I replied, prepared to resume our battle from below. I pointed to the damaged banister, along with several large holes in the marble walls. A doorway looked like an armored tank drove through it, save for the strange decay around the edges. "Whoever did this is *your* friend, *not* mine! Only a diabolical assbag like yourself would...."

Then it hit me. Hard.

The demons, the destruction that was more of a molecular shift than a hole caused by a powerful force smashing into an immovable object—It all began to gel together in my mind.

FGR technology. Only a fusion generator/reconfiguration beam device could do this! Oh, holy shit!

Viktor Kaslow.

My worst nemesis ever, and one I assumed became dinner to a host of voracious entities known as Bochicha's Emissaries, was back. He must've turned the tables on the Colombian deity and its angels, and then escaped to our reality.

How lovely.

I shuddered, recognizing Krontos' little dig about another person being better at dimension manipulation than any of us, while also managing to confiscate the Stutthof-Auschwitz coin with relatively little effort. Now this person successfully invaded Krontos' home and seemingly had gained the upper hand on him, too.

Lord help us all if the two should ever be united as one.

"So, you do know who is responsible for the destruction of my beautiful home?" The wicked smile returned to Krontos' face, and he nodded as if reviewing the rush of random thoughts swirling in my mind. "I might consider such an alignment, if not for the destructive mayhem this Kaslow has caused in other dimensions. He is a brute, having no regard for the proper sequence of things."

"Isn't that a 'pot calling the kettle black' kind of thing?" I said, realizing I wouldn't have long to rescue my family and friends if my Russian enemy sought to settle our personal score in the cold wee hours after Halloween. "Insane tyrants are all the same."

No, really they're not. Similar, maybe, but like anyone else, bad guys have their individual quirks that make it fairly easy to rank one above another when stacking them up. But debating the sins and merits of Krontos and Kaslow wasn't why I said what I did. I had just stepped toward the room with the blown out doorway, trying to hone in on my coin's call, as well as seeking clues where my loved ones were presently held. The signal grew weaker until I headed for the stairs to the third floor.

My left arm began to tingle, where the earlier sensation had been more of a bodily awareness. I thought about the room holding Krontos' Nazi paraphernalia, and in particular, the cobalt glowing sun crosses. Avoiding the obvious connection any longer was foolish, even if the coins were not involved. The room was the logical choice to resume my search.

"Where in the hell do you think you're going?" Krontos picked up his pace.

"I guess you'll need to keep up if you really want to know," I said, grasping the ice-cold banister and bolting into the dimness above while a myriad of new fears bombarded me. Igniting Krontos' ire was the least of them, as the presence of Kaslow and the demons that craved the sweetness of human flesh were bigger concerns.

The dimness deepened toward pitch black as I stepped onto the third floor. I tried to remember the relic room's location, ever-fearful Krontos might move it somewhere else by reality shift or sorcery. Not to mention the possibility Kaslow had found it already. Thankfully, a soft blue glow emanated from an area to my left, and when I encountered a door that opened with little resistance, I released a huge sigh of relief.

I stepped inside, surprised to find a warm breeze embracing me—so unlike anywhere else in the castle at present. But the glowing sun crosses were barely visible, as compared to my earlier visit.

"The reunion of three coins was your responsibility, Judas," said Krontos from behind me. Several wall torches ignited simultaneously, filling the room with soft luminance. "But if my assumption is correct about your friend, Viktor Kaslow, then all will be well. I will have my Trinity of Death again and

Kaslow will have you. I think that works out well for everyone!"

"What about Beatrice, Amy, Alistair, Roderick, and Cedric?" I purposely named them all, in the faint hope they could hear me bartering for their lives. "I'd go willingly to Kaslow in a trade, as long as they are allowed to return home safely. I want you to personally see them home in one piece and assure me they will be allowed to live out their days in happiness."

"What? How is that supposed to work, Judas?" he said, snickering while he regarded me with disdain. "Even my disciples in the Third Reich understood goodness delivered without a wicked deed to cap things off was a project incomplete. What I can promise you is they will endure suffering beyond what they could ever anticipate, with enough discomfort to ensure they hardly think about you."

He smiled almost sweetly. Perhaps if he had delivered his condemnation without such relish and anticipation of my loved ones' suffering, I might've let it ride. Not likely, but possible, since I was without a clue where to check for my coins—which I had begun to see as the likely keys to our salvation. If they had somehow been transformed into the sun crosses as their present state, how could I possibly change them back to what they once were? Cursed as an immortal to live out my days without any way to permanently kill me, I could never thwart someone with Krontos' or Kaslow's vision. They would merely brush me aside on the way to wreaking havoc upon the world.

While thinking along these lines, a sharp pain entered my back, came out through my abdomen after piercing my liver, and exited from my back. I stumbled as I turned around. Krontos was there. A wide grin stretched his wrinkled face, and he held a medieval battleaxe in his hands, dripping with my blood along its tip.

"Kaslow won't come out to play, I fear, unless I give him an invitation," he advised, as I fell to my knees. A vital organ had been compromised and if he struck me again—say in the heart or head—my recovery would be dubious at best. "Hold still and be a good boy... maybe your God will surprise you by letting you inside St. Peter's Gates."

More laughter. Mean and robust—enough to make me briefly consider whether Kaslow was truly more evil than Krontos. But one thing was painfully clear. With so many different options of how to kill me, whether natural or supernatural, I was running out of time. I had to make a move, and it had to be the right one.

I collapsed on the floor as Krontos prepared to finish me off with the axe. Lining the weapon up with my neck for an apparent decapitation, as he raised the axe to take a swing I mustered the last of my reserves and rolled away from him to the platform holding the crosses. Before he could stop me, I reached up and grabbed both crosses, pulling them down as I fell on my back.

It was a desperate move, knowing I'd have no way to transform the crosses into the coins, if that was in fact their original state. Each cross was at least one hundred times bigger than a silver shekel, and all either item had in common was the silver content and the mysterious blue glow.

But as my hands were losing their grip on the crosses, and my head grew light from the glow's sudden rise in intensity, I noticed two small silver disks resting inside the ethereal blue flame.

My previous mistake was to assume the coins would be resting on something or lying in a box, perhaps stored in cerecloth. I never considered the damned things would be floating, just inside the top of each sun cross.

Krontos screamed, realizing I could see the coins, and warning me not to pursue the powerful thought in my head that followed my surprised gasp. He failed to prevent my hands from grasping the coins. I knew I'd be powerless to fight him off, and my death remained likely—especially given the rage when he reached me.

I felt his fingers tearing at my hands, along with the sting from voracious bites in his desperation to get me to release my tenacious grip. But the painful attacks were soon replaced by the vision I had come to expect with each redeemed coin. Only this time, it was far worse than anticipated. Had I known what would happen, I would've grasped one coin instead of two.

For those unfamiliar, in the past when I've touched my blood coins, I am taken back in time to Jesus Christ's arrest and execution—forced to relive the torture, anguish, and full realization of suffering He would soon endure on the cross. Whether or not that included the terrible weight from the world's sins is not for me to judge or expound upon. What I've experienced is the heavy sadness and indescribable sense of guilt for my role in His betrayal. Intensified with each coin I recover.

But now it was beyond that. Two coins together provided a hostile experience more emotionally painful than anything I could've ever imagined.

Though it lasted under a minute, the event will stay with me for the rest of my earthly days. The vision suddenly shifted, and instead of me observing Jesus from behind the woman's veil—Mary's hijab—I saw things from where Jesus stood. The labored breaths, taste of blood in my mouth, and blurred vision from the bleeding crown of thorns—I experienced it all! I *felt* what He felt, and it truly was too much to bear.

Immortal Tyranny

Something no human being could endure, it was almost as bad for this immortal. When it ended and I was pulled back to the present, I could only watch Krontos pummel my prone body with an attack as vicious as any territorial baboon. In retrospect, I believe he thought I died. Otherwise, I suppose he would've clawed out my defenseless eyes, or worse.

My eyes fluttered. He launched into a vile tirade with more anti-Semitic insults, adding references to what he witnessed his SS men do to women in the presence of their tormented husbands, forced to watch. Surely these comments were intended to be a preview of what awaited my Beatrice and Alistair's bride-to-be, while the two of us watched—just as our Jewish brethren were forced to do seventy years earlier.

Unable to move, to my horror the ironclad grip I had on my coins began to loosen. I couldn't hold on, and I watched Krontos' expression of vehement hatred turn to enraptured surprise.

"Ah, that's better," he said, his tone peaceful as he reached for the coins. "Once I free them from your defiled fingers, I will deal with you once and for all, Yehudah. This should only take a moment... *Owww!*"

His touch had merely grazed the one in my left palm after prying my fingers free, perhaps expecting the coin to drop into his open palm. However, it remained attached to my palm, as if glued to the skin. It was the same for the coin in my right hand, and a louder cry of pain resulted when Krontos grabbed it. He jerked his hand back, as if he touched a fiery coal instead.

"Damn you, Judas!" he shouted. "I'll kill you if I must—let *go!*"

"I'm... I'm not holding onto them," I responded, weakly, still recovering from my most recent coin-holding experience. Something else was different, and difficult to define at first. "Honestly, I'm not."

Immortal Tyranny

True. Both were adhered to my palms by some other force.

"Let them go!" he shrieked.

"I can't!" I shouted back. A fresh surge of energy flowed through me. "You'll have to kill me to have a chance at them, Krontos. Do you know what will happen then? You've heard the legends, right?"

A sudden cloud passed over his countenance, and his hatred softened.

"That's right," I said, trying to keep my excitement down. "You kill me while holding these coins—or rather, while they're holding onto me—and you'll likely never see either one again. Wherever I go, they'll automatically come with me."

If I didn't have so much riding on the line, I might've smiled at the look of dumbfounded horror on the fiend's face. He backed away, nodding his understanding. I thought he might give me enough space to stand up. But a moment later the rage was back full force. He dove at me once more, clawing at my hands to try and tear the coins out.

A disastrous mistake on his part.

I expected Krontos to shriek in pain from touching the coins again. He surely expected it, too. What neither of us anticipated was the sudden surge of blue flames engulfing his hands. The flames swept up his arms and traversed quickly across the monster's torso. As soon as the matching streams met near his heart, the angry blue fire burst into hundreds of new flames that engulfed his entire body.

He became a writhing torch, wailing in high-pitched shrieks unheard since his days as a squalling infant eight hundred years ago. The flames didn't consume the body, and Krontos couldn't free himself from this spell, despite waving his arms wildly in desperate attempts at an incantation. Nothing could save him. In the end, a cruel man had found equally cruel justice.

Chapter Eighteen

As Krontos began his new existence as an eternal fire, the blue sheen covering the shekels in my hands faded to where it was barely detectable. I slipped the coins into separate pockets, fearful of inadvertently bringing the Silver Trinity of Death to life if they came in close contact with the Dragon Coin in my wallet.

My strength fully restored, I needed to find the others. Find them before Viktor Kaslow showed up. During the latest battle with Krontos, I glimpsed one of Bochicha's Emissaries in the room's doorway. The demon brought its immense body and wingspan into the room for only a moment before disappearing. Surely by now it had reported my present location to Kaslow, or perhaps the Russian already knew. It wasn't like Krontos and I pantomimed our contest.

The biggest challenge in locating my companions was where to begin the search. I didn't sense anyone near the relic room, and yet I had the distinct feeling I'd find them on the third floor. Krontos' pitiful screams echoed behind me as I stepped into the darkened hallway. Despite the valid fear of an unseen attack, I focused on Beatrice, since she came to mind first. I pictured her laughing merrily in an attempt to cheer up Amy and Alistair, and I prayed the impression would soon be confirmed.

Immortal Tyranny

I crept quietly, pulled to explore the rooms to my left instead of those along the right. Powerful wings fluttering near the gallery to my left briefly distracted me, though it remained virtually impossible to make out anything in the darkness beyond the relic room, where the blue glow from Krontos writhing body seeped into the hallway. The scrutiny from encroaching watchful eyes from beyond that point grew strong, and I prepared myself for the bloodcurdling screeches I remembered from Bolivia.

Meanwhile, I diligently traced my fingers along the walls, trying to remember the contours of the marble and dormant torch holders, hoping to find the door that called to me. Since my intuitions were sometimes flawed, I prayed I wasn't wasting precious time exploring a dead end path. Strangely, this felt different than the hit-miss hunches I usually fell into.

Not this time. They're here, Judas.... Somewhere close.

More fluttering sounds behind me indicated a small crowd was forming near the gallery. I tried not to think of the feeding frenzy that might start at any moment. Immortal or not, I would be just an appetizer for the bigger prize of human flesh presently hidden nearby.

The wall gave way to a doorframe, and my pulse quickened. But the latch was securely locked with what felt like a skeleton keyhole. I stooped to see if I could make out anything through the tiny hole, and whispered my wife's name.

No response from beyond the door. But claws scraped against the hall's marble floor, sending a warning my way. Bochicha's fallen angels were getting antsy.

I didn't have long, and began to doubt my gut instincts when the next door I encountered was just like the first one. Very soon I might be faced with plowing through a demon horde to get to the other side and continue my search there.

Nearing the last room on this side of the hall, I prepared to investigate the keyhole.

As I stooped, I heard voices coming from the room directly across from me. I paused to listen, and heard them again.

Roderick? Saying something to Cedric... I heard his name. Shit! Better hurry!

I scurried across the floor, for a moment forgetting my brooding observers down the hall. Unlike the other doors, this one was unlocked. The room was dark and the voices immediately stopped when I pushed the door ajar. Was this a lingering trick from Krontos? A possible trap in the event I gained the upper hand against him?

I would soon find out.

The sound of flapping wings approached. I pushed the door fully open and slipped inside, unprepared to face whatever waited in the frigid blackness. A complete act of faith—or foolishness, depending on the perspective—I set the iron latch behind me and stood... listening.

All was still, deathly quiet. I detected something else.

Breathing. Air taken in and released in uneven bursts. Without time to better brace myself for whatever shared the room with me, I used the flashlight from my cell phone to illuminate my surroundings.

I gasped.

Roderick and Cedric were bound to wooden chairs to my right, and to my left sat Beatrice, Amy, and Alistair. All were gagged and disheveled. But at least they were alive and appeared relatively uninjured.

Once Beatrice recognized me, she squealed through the gag over her mouth. Everyone followed her excited reaction except Roderick, who appeared exhausted, though he eyed me gratefully.

"We don't have much time," I whispered, tearing the bonds from Cedric and Roderick, so they could take care of Amy and Alistair while I attended to Beatrice.

My love wrapped her arms around my neck as I lifted her from the chair. Trembling, she fought admirably to control her tears. I held her tightly, comforting her with soothing whispered promises of protection while affirming my undying love for her. But as this was not the time to celebrate anything, I led everyone to the doorway, which suddenly splintered.

Holy shit—I'm too late!

"Not yet, my brother," said Roderick, answering my panicked thoughts and taking my phone to shine a light across the room. A thick windowsill peered out from a heavy tapestry. "Most of the castle's rooms have windows."

He smiled weakly, hardly enjoying the joke at my expense, as we urged the others to make a dash for the window.

"Alistair, help me tear this sucker down!" shouted Cedric, pulling on one end of the thick, ornate tapestry that had successfully camouflaged the window's presence. "We'll have to get Beatrice and Amy out of here first, then the rest of us. William, you'll have to be last, since you heal the quickest between you and Roderick."

I was about to concur, but a heavier crash behind us tore open a sizeable gash in the door. The restraint wouldn't last much longer.

"Can you grip the fabric while we lower you down?" I asked Beatrice, after throwing a chair through the window, destroying stained glass panes several centuries old. Krontos would be most unhappy, I'm sure, if he didn't have much bigger fish to fry at the moment. "I'm sorry I can't make this any easier."

Roderick and Alistair were rolling up the tapestry while Alistair prepared to secure the edge with the window's splintered frame. Fortunately, this ancient tapestry from what appeared to be the Ottoman Empire period was roughly a dozen feet longer than the window's twenty-foot width. Still, considering the forty-foot drop from the window to the front courtyard below, everyone would have to drop the last ten feet to reach the unforgiving cobblestones below.

Provided we got everyone out in time.

"William, this ain't the time for lovey-dovey shit!" warned Cedric, as the first demon talon successfully made it through the door's wound, clawing at the iron restraint bar. "Get your wife's ass over here, now!"

He and Roderick tossed the tapestry through the window, where gusts of wind added additional peril to getting down. Not to mention, once the tapestry's surface was exposed to the deepening chill outside the castle, it would be much more difficult to cling to. Without a moment to lose, I kissed my wife and lifted her onto the tapestry while the other guys held the top of it to give additional support.

Beatrice slid down to the bottom, uttering a startled yelp as she instinctively clung to the fraying tassels before dropping to the ground. I braced myself for the sound of breaking bones, but she landed with a slight thud on her butt. Still, I worried until she stood up and waved she was okay.

Next came Amy, who seemed to draw confidence from watching Beatrice. If not for the sound of the iron restraint falling to the floor below us, I might've drawn encouragement from Amy's quick descent to the ground.

But it was too late to wait on anyone else to go down the safe way.

"Rod, we're out of time, and you know what we have to do, right?"

"Indeed. I hate it when things work out like this." He grimaced.

"What in the hell are you two talking about? Quit jacking around—*Huh?!*"

Cedric's surprise was matched by Alistair's. As a horde of demons flew toward us, I grabbed Alistair and Roderick grabbed Cedric. We dove out the window, careful to twist our bodies to land with the least damage to our passengers. I sent a silent prayer heavenward that Alistair and Cedric would join Beatrice and Amy unscathed, and Roderick's injuries wouldn't prevent him from hobbling to the car. As for me, by now most everyone knows it takes a much more severe fall to bring me anymore than a few minutes of discomfort. Although, snapping bones back into place to aid the healing process is not usually a pretty sight.

I landed on the edge of my feet and rolled. Alistair received a few scrapes from the cobblestones. Despite momentary agonizing pain from shattered legs, feet, and several vertebrae in my lower back, by the time I stumbled to where Amy and Beatrice waited I had mostly healed.

As I feared, Roderick got the worst of it. A broken femur and ankle in one leg, along with two ruptured disks in his lower back. Injuries that might take several hours to heal, and a day or two before he walked pain free again. It's the only time I feel guilty about my body's ability to heal in a matter of minutes. But if he ever tired of his long existence on Earth, Roderick would be free to leave on his own accord. Unlike me.

My druid buddy limped gingerly as far as he could make it, just beyond the entrance steps. Alistair and Cedric lifted him on to their shoulders, and I gathered our ladies, with the intent of reaching the car before we encountered any other trouble. However, Bochicha's Emissaries circled above us, and their numbers had increased tenfold. There would be no way to outrun them to Krontos' Mercedes, parked roughly a football field's distance away.

"What do we do now?!" Amy cried. *"Oh my God—here they come!"*

In the fading moonlight, the demons' hideousness became clearly defined. Their deep ebony skin was translucent, with a putrid pink substance pulsing like blood between powerful muscles. Their eyes morphed from green to red, and their wide mouths were filled with long razor-like teeth. All were at least ten feet in height, and several feet wide, with bat-like wings.

Beyond ugly and, unfortunately, immortal as the Lord's angels. Once angels themselves long ago, they fell from grace when The Children of Elohim were cast off the earth. But that's a story for another day.

Did I mention they have an insatiable craving for human flesh? The Essenes in Bolivia told us last year they had witnessed men devoured whole by these merciless creatures.

Despite such endearing qualities, I briefly considered making a dash on my own to reach the car and bring it back to pick everyone else up. But any escape was futile. Besides, Roderick had the keys to the Mercedes, last I checked.

I gathered Beatrice and Amy close to me, pushing them behind my legs while I prepared to fight to the death—certainly a quicker one compared to what Krontos had in mind. Roderick tried to do the same thing for Alistair and Cedric, but he couldn't stand, crying out in agony when he attempted to balance himself without anyone's help.

Oddly, the demons' notorious screeches had been silent until then. But as if making up for lost time, their eerie and physically painful calls filled the air above.

"I guess it's meal time, and we're it," lamented Cedric. "I don't suppose you've got a trusty old spell you can throw on 'em, Roderick?"

"I wish I did have something," said Roderick, sadly. "I have nothing. I have…."

Immortal Tyranny

We all heard what drew Roderick's gaze back to the castle, and it quieted the demons' cries. The menacing horde turned their gazes toward the castle as well, toward one of the spires atop the structure. A large human being stood at the edge of the sloping roof, wearing a dark green trench coat and carrying what looked like a cache of military-grade weapons strapped to his back.

The figure laughed, and though it started out sounding diabolical it became almost jolly in timbre.

"Well, hello, William Barrow! Have you missed me?"

Normally, this would be where something relatively clever flowed out of my mouth. But after dealing with a steady emotional assault over the past few months, from ominous roses to Holocaust tragedies to finally besting the sorcerer who aided two of my deaths and prepared to deliver another, all I could do was shake my head in response.

Not to mention Viktor Kaslow's release from Bochicha's version of hell, and the fact I could almost see his smirk from where we were gathered below his present perch. Knowing his penchant for wickedness that rivaled Krontos, my night couldn't get much worse.

"Oh, William, William...."

The Russian sounded compassionate... almost. Whatever ability had allowed me to find my family a short while earlier also made it possible to clearly see the diabolical wheels turning inside this evil brute's head. I would've given most anything to not see what lurked in Kaslow's wicked heart and the schemes planned for me and my family.

An immortal unmatched by any that Roderick or I had ever encountered during our two-millennium stay on Earth, I expected him to jump down and join us. Instead, he preferred to climb down the walls, using the dormant vines and gutters to reach the ground in a matter of seconds. He stood to face us, and we all huddled closer to one another.

The Tree of Life's crystal buried in his chest pulsed unnaturally, as always. Up close, the blonde Russian's enormous ripped muscles and chiseled features looked more unreal than the last time we squared off in Bolivia. His intense steel blue eyes were colder than the air around us. Rocket launchers and the miniature version of an FGR peered out from the weapon sack on his back. Like a comic book super villain. The biggest differences from the last time we faced off were a number of long shark-bite scars along his face, neck, and arms—as if he had fallen into predatory Amazon waters—and the presence of his newfound army.

"If only you knew what it took to win them over," he said, coolly, motioning to the demons hovering nearby. Like most immortals I've known, he carried the ability to see inside my head. I almost smiled at the irony that I could finally read his thoughts, too. "They tried to eat me first, William, and I owe *all* of that to you. Can you even begin to imagine the fun things I've been planning for our reunion? Hmmm?"

He wasn't kidding. Everything from cannibalizing me, slowly, and then chopping up my kin and friends to be fed as treats to the demonic army he now controlled.

He laughed more boisterously and stepped toward us, eyeing me angrily. This wasn't going to be pretty.

"On second thought, I think I'll feed you all to my new friends whole, starting with the troublesome Amy Golden Eagle first!"

He reached for Amy, grasping her arm and yanking her toward him like a rag doll before any of us could react. Alistair launched himself at Kaslow, and found himself in a strangle hold next to his beloved. My heart sunk at the prospects they would both be dead in the next few minutes. I had to think of something fast, and yet, I had nothing to bargain with.... Or, did I?

"Kaslow, are you content for Krontos Lazarevic to be the most powerful man the world has ever known?"

He looked at me with brows furrowed, and I could see new wheels turning in his head. The Tree of Life's permanent tonic in his system had completely rewired his mind to where he was so much more than a cunning KGB officer. I had no doubt he could now hold his own with any mathematician or astrophysicist on the planet. But the primitive need for conquest overrode all else.

"You mean the burning torch upstairs—that Krontos?"

My kid was turning blue. I had less than a minute to work a miracle.

"Yes."

He chuckled meanly.

"Humor me for just a moment," I said, with my son's life ebbing away by the second. "He is that way because my coins that once were part of the Silver Trinity of Death caused it to happen. The man who inspired and dictated the rise of the Third Reich is now my bitch!"

Time was just about out. But I couldn't panic. I couldn't even send a prayer for mercy on behalf of my boy.

I saw the flicker in Kaslow's eye.

"Release my son *now,* and I'll hand them over to you," I said, keeping my tone as steady as I could, ready to die inside at the moment Alistair expired. "If you don't release him, I swear to God I will take these coins with me and you'll *never* rule the world!"

Did I mention this is Viktor's ultimate goal these days? It was in fact what he wanted when he pursued me to South America a year ago. I hoped I hadn't misread him, as what else would his presence in Hungary mean? Why take the one coin that would give Krontos such a reign, unless he wanted it for himself?

It made sense. But not necessarily perfect sense. Not if Viktor didn't bite, and I lost my only beloved son in the process.

Afraid to hold this fiend in my gaze, I did so anyway. He smirked and dropped Alistair. Beatrice ran to our boy while he struggled to breathe. He reached up to grab Amy, the love of his life, drawing a snicker from Kaslow, who pulled her out of Alistair's reach.

"She needs to be a part of the deal, too, since my son's happiness is what will ensure his survival. And, his survival is what will get you the coins," I said. "It's as simple as that."

"Things are *never* that simple, William!" he shot back.

But to my surprise, he dropped Amy to the ground. She landed hard, and Alistair scurried to her side, tenderly cradling her shaking body in his arms. Beatrice joined them in sobbing like babies. My aching heart broke, and I hated Kaslow more than ever.

"Hand me the coins," he said gruffly.

He reached out his large paw, and I knew then if the coins brought a different reaction than the one that happened to Krontos, my family and friends would be murdered horribly before me. Or, if the sorcerer's spell no longer affected the coins, our fate could be even worse. But, to resist further meant testing this supreme miscreant's patience to the point he would kill first and face regret later.

I pulled out the coins from my pockets. I purposely blocked out the mental image of the Dragon Coin in my wallet. After all, why give this fiend four coins to work with when three was bad enough? Before Kaslow moved to take them from my hands, I was already leaving the present day reality for the moment I have relived more than I care to calculate. I knew it

Immortal Tyranny

would be very bad again... reliving more of the terrifying torture and crucifixion moments from Jesus Christ's perspective.

But before my spirit was lifted away, I saw the look of surprise and horror on Kaslow's face. Something was happening to him, and whatever it was he didn't like it. Didn't care for it one bit.

I heard Beatrice somewhere above me as I fell into the spiraling light that always takes me back for the most intense episodes of reliving Jesus' betrayal. She was trying to tell me something. Something about love forever... and then I heard screeches. Or was it screaming?

Whatever it was, I prayed fervently my family and friends would still be there—whole and happy—whenever I returned. And, that this time when I'm face to face with Jesus, He would truly know I mean it when I repent for all the wrong I've done.

Especially, in regard to what I've done to Him.

Chapter Nineteen

"Well I'll be damned.... Looks like our sleeping beauty is waking up!"

Cedric chuckled as he said this, and as I opened my eyes I thought perhaps I was dreaming. Dreaming about sitting in the Mercedes SUV's middle seat, with a smiling Beatrice to my left, and my ornery former CIA pal in the front passenger seat. Cedric peered at me from above the neck rest, holding a slim panatela in his right hand. The passenger window was cracked slightly to allow the smoke to escape.

"I thought you gave those up forever?" I said, my throat feeling parched. "They'll kill you."

"Seems like everything these days can kill us," he said, offering me a generous, impish smile. "Just grease the palms of the FDA, and yesterday's poison becomes today's delicacy and poster child for a healthy, long life. But I ain't planning on dying anytime soon."

Beatrice laughed, and I realized she had been affectionately stroking my hair for a while. No longer disheveled, she looked refreshed and calm. The love exuding toward me was powerful—something I had always known about her, but I could literally *feel* it pulsing now. So vibrant and everlasting.

Immortal Tyranny

It was indeed a dream!

"No, William... this is quite real," said Roderick, from the driver's seat. He seemed almost completely recovered from the injuries sustained at Krontos' castle. "I must admit I thought you had lost your mind when you offered the coins to Viktor Kaslow. But it worked."

"It worked a helluva lot better than any of us expected, Pops," said Alistair, from somewhere behind me. I tried to raise myself to look in his direction, but an unfamiliar lightheadedness prevented me from doing it just yet.

"Welcome back, William," said Amy, sitting next to Alistair. Her voice sounded as if it came from where Alistair sat. Must be ignoring seatbelt requirements. "We've got a lot to tell you."

"Yes, we do, darling," said Beatrice, leaning over to kiss me. "You had us very worried."

Suddenly, I heard voices. Not audible ones, but a litany of silent thoughts. They all came from within the vehicle.

"I would say welcome to the club," said Roderick, glancing back at me. "But until you learn how to filter other people's thoughts, you will have bursts of what I like to call 'psychic episodes', where you hear nothing but a stream of chatter. Like what you're hearing at present, correct?"

I nodded, giving my wife a sheepish look in regard to the physically amorous thought I just picked up from her.

"Part of the divine now lives within you, my brother," continued Roderick. "I say it's high time you could relate to my malady." He grinned, and returned his attention to the road.

"Isn't there a way to make it stop?"

"No. But you can learn to dial in to the most pleasant frequencies, and in time you'll train yourself to ignore the unwanted ones," he advised.

Immortal Tyranny

He glanced at Cedric, who eyed us both suspiciously. I bet he was over the moon about this development, knowing how much he hated Roderick's insights into my unspoken thoughts. Now he might never know we're having a mental conversation, unless Roderick or I announce it.

Roderick nodded. "Yes, won't that be fun? Anyway, if you ever feel overwhelmed by your new ability, keep in mind most human beings hear a steady ring or hum emanating from inside their heads. If they concentrate for a moment, they can hear it clearly. I guarantee most would tell you they hardly noticed it before."

"Sounds like bullshit," said Cedric.

"No, remember? *Smells* like bullshit," I corrected him.

"Oh, wow—it's true. I hear a hum!" Amy sounded excited. "How about you, Ali?"

"I don't know... I don't hear anything."

But he did hear something... just not defined enough to where he was comfortable sharing that information. At least that's what his thoughts told me.

"Hey, hon'... would you like something to eat?" asked Beatrice. "We've got some snacks in the car. Or, we can stop someplace. What's the next city on the way to Berlin, Roderick?"

"We're coming up on Dresden, and should reach Berlin before dark," he said. "We took a more direct route to return to Berlin from Budapest, William, after we returned there from Krontos' castle. We made it to Prague just before lunchtime, but decided to keep driving. We were hoping you would awaken soon."

I looked out the window next to me. The sun was shining, and melting snow covered both sides of the highway. It looked like early afternoon.

Immortal Tyranny

"So, I've been out since…. Wait, is it November first or the second?"

"It's still the first," said Cedric. "The day after Halloween, and y'all are still as strange as ever."

His eyes were aglow with playfulness, and he blew a stream of smoke that veered to the small crease at the top of his window.

"The last thing I remember was Kaslow," I said. "He was taking my coins from me."

Until that moment, I couldn't recall anything beyond being pulled down the familiar spiraling path through the centuries, a journey that always brought me back to the most heinous moment in my existence. My betrayal of Jesus Christ.

But beyond my usual arrival points of either Simon Zelotes' home in Jerusalem or in the crowd gathered around the temple fortress, better known as the Antonia, my mind was a blank slate. Then, suddenly, the events hidden from my awareness began to pour in rapidly. I soon discovered why my mind shut down and tried to bury this particular experience.

I knew the handling of multiple blood coins could bring dire consequences, and I dreaded a deeper plunge into the Lord's psyche. It felt wrong the first time it happened, as if I were stealing secrets from The Almighty that no man is ever entitled to know. But there I was, experiencing Christ's physical and emotional torment from His perspective while still human. Fortunately, the first coin event in the relic room ended mercifully before I was forced to share what Jesus endured after receiving His sentence from Pontius Pilate. The brutal second round of beatings and other unspeakable humiliation omitted from the Gospels would soon commence, and they wouldn't end until Jesus' crucifixion later in the day.

Some may wonder why I omit the Sanhedrin's trial from the evening before. It was a worse mockery of justice than the single-man court under Pontius Pilate the following morning. The Sanhedrin event was informal and quick. Caiaphas had already received approval to bring Jesus before Pilate on political charges of insurrection, so the Jewish hierarchy held off on beating Him, worried they might be seen as a bigger threat to the Pax Romana than a nomad mystic claiming to be the long awaited King of the Jews.

I had no idea just how fortunate I was in my initial viewing of this snippet from long ago, a swift experience that left me momentarily defenseless against Krontos. Less than an hour later, when surrendering my coins to Kaslow, I was forced to endure the entire sequence of events.

As an unwilling voyeur, I shared Jesus' agony and profound sorrow from the moment the temple guards and Roman troops arrived at Simon's courtyard, and it didn't end until He was nailed to the cross at Golgotha. The Lord's anxiety steadily worsened, though His faith never wavered. Faith, as the belief in things unseen, doesn't mean totally ignoring the present circumstances and attendant emotions. It is courage more than confidence.

The beatings from the Roman soldiers worsened; they seemed to take great pleasure in making it nearly impossible for Jesus to drag the cross through the streets of Jerusalem. Of course, most everyone knows all this and how things turned out. But they might be curious to know how the Romans' hatred of the Jewish race had a profound affect on Him. I could hear the silent prayers to The Almighty for mercy towards *them*.

And I saw the future through His eyes. Even then, He knew another nation like Rome would one day rise and share the same opinions of the outward world. This new tyrant would focus on the same efficient ways to kill, and employ extreme cruelty to ensure compliance by the masses they conquered.

Immortal Tyranny

Heil Hitler to you, Roma.

If the world knew what I had already known for so long, that it was Caesar's men and not the Jews who killed Jesus, how would the good folk of Italy be seen today?

"Hon, are you all right?" Beatrice nudged my shoulder gently.

"Huh? Oh, sorry... I was thinking about Kaslow." It was intended to be a white lie to protect her from worry, but Roderick shot a knowing look through the rearview mirror, subtly shaking his head.

"We should forget about him," she said, resolutely, her tone solemn. "For now."

"What became of him? I mean... how did we escape this time?"

I needed to know. And, as far as the experience of reliving Jesus' last day and a half as a mortal man, I decided not to allow myself the horror of going through it any further than I already had. Some things are better left forgotten, or at least kept far away from the forefront of our awareness. The Passion Play, which I had a hand in creating, needed to remain the watered down version embraced by millions. For me there wasn't a choice, unless I wanted to be a permanent liability to those I loved. Especially true if Kaslow presumably was still on the loose.

"You forget we've had your 'the Italians killed Jesus' debate before, Judas," Roderick chided, cheerfully. "Just as you've changed over the years, so can anyone else. But to answer your spoken question.... Your blood coins ignited Kaslow's hands, and he threw the glowing shekels back at you. It didn't prevent the flames from climbing his arms. One of the larger demons rescued him, and we watched the horde fly into a wormhole in the early morning sky, similar to the escape route he used in Bolivia. You had lost consciousness, and

Beatrice and I focused on saving you while the others kept an eye out for Kaslow's return."

"We were so worried, my love." Beatrice wrapped her arm inside mine, scooting closer. "But we couldn't stay there and wait for you to wake up."

"Or go back inside that hellhole," added Amy.

"But we still weren't out of the woods, man," said Cedric, pausing to take a longer drag from his slim cigar. "The jokers who brought us to the castle in the first place... what were their names?"

"Arso, Jevrem, and Gajo," I said. "Sounds like three thoroughbreds running at Preakness."

"Not any I'd ever bet on." He joined me in chuckling for a moment. "They pursued us down the mountain in another Mercedes. I've gotta give props to Roderick for keeping us on the road while those assholes tried to shoot out the tires. They didn't make it through one of the tighter curves as we neared the main highway. Otherwise...."

He didn't finish. Nor did he need to, as I glimpsed what he saw earlier that day, where gunfire just missed the tires and did a number on the trunk and fender. Good thing this wasn't the rental we had to return. Which inspired more questions.

"Save your strength, William," said Roderick. "We'll rest up when we return to the Esplanade in Berlin. Our flight's been changed to nine-forty tonight."

"Why the urgency to get out of here this evening?" I asked, unable to sort through everyone's random thoughts for a clear answer. In truth, my unfamiliarity with reading thought streams had given me a slight headache. Yes, I know... it would pass in a moment. But irritation at the prospect of this experience being much worse—especially in a busy airport—was enough for me to try Roderick's advice on how to shut it down.

"Kaslow is likely to avoid us for awhile, I imagine, after nearly becoming barbeque, and... and, where are the coins?"

Sudden panic at not knowing the coins' whereabouts deepened when I found my pockets were empty, other than my wallet. The Dragon Coin's steady hum was barely audible, so I left the wallet alone.

"Cedric has one and I've got the other," Roderick advised. "After what happened back there, it makes sense to not have these particular coins kept in one place."

"True." Relieved, I began to relax. But something nagged at my mind. Something about security of the other coins in Sedona, Arizona.

"Aren't we going to tell Pops the latest news about Krontos?" Alistair asked.

I felt him lean closer to Beatrice and me, and heard the thoughts feeding his anxiety. It was profound worry about the other coins. Why? ...Then I saw the image in his head, which matched another in Beatrice's. Two views of the same event.

"Krontos might've escaped," said Roderick. "Impossible to know for sure, but it does seem likely."

"Hell, man, there ain't no denying the guy we saw herding sheep near the Czech Republic's border was him," Cedric insisted. "Dude was a dead ringer, and we all saw the way he looked at us, right?"

"Like he knew us," Alistair agreed. "Little guy with white hair and that same annoying smile. If it wasn't him, somewhere down the line these two guys are related. I guarantee it."

"Probably inbred," said Cedric.

Amy and Beatrice added their agreement, and I now understood the urgency of leaving Berlin and Europe that night. I also saw what everyone had witnessed in the late morning fog as the Mercedes prepared to cross the Czech/German border. The wee shepherd moving sheep across the road caused the car to stop and wait until all the animals had safely crossed the highway. He eyed the vehicle's occupants slyly, as if he wanted them to notice him. Once they did, he smiled broadly, nodded slightly, and moved to the other side of the road while never taking his eyes off the car.

As Roderick sought to put as much distance between the little man and us, before he disappeared from view, the shepherd nodded his head in exaggerated movements. As if to say, "I'm back!"

No one talked about it, out of fear of Krontos' possible revenge—if it was him. And, if it wasn't? They worried anyway.

"So, now you know," said Roderick. "We'll head back to the States, grab your coins, and search for someplace new to live."

"Sounds perfectly lovely…. Here we go again, huh?" I sighed, suddenly feeling exhausted. "Am I to assume Krontos shifted into one of his alternate existences, then? Taking over the poor shepherd's life and leaving the poor sot to burn in his stead forever? Nice guy. Truly."

It was one of those moments where you had to laugh to keep from crying. Would there never be an end to this shit?

"Unfortunately, yes," said Roderick. "We need to assume this is the case, while hoping it isn't. But if it is? Then we will have much bigger—and meaner—fish to fry than just Viktor Kaslow. So, we have much to discuss on the flight back to America."

Indeed. Perhaps the right perspective would be to count the blessings I did have, instead of worrying about what could go wrong. After all, it was out of our hands, one way or another. Besides, in the end, things might turn out better than feared.

I had my beloved family and friends. I had my destiny. Despite not knowing how much time I had left to appreciate them both, I had that day to cherish the one and to reflect upon the other.

I smiled at Beatrice, pulling her closer. Her eyes were on fire and her countenance aglow. My heart felt as if it would burst from devotion, watching her. She snuggled against my chest until her eyes closed.

Protection and comfort, we both needed it.

We *all* needed it.

It's what I sent as a silent prayer to The Almighty. May His mercy prevail, and may freedom from tyranny be our miracle.

The End

To be continued in:
Immortal Pyramid
The Judas Chronicles, Book Six
Available now

About the Author

Aiden James is the bestselling author of *Cades Cove*, *The Judas Chronicles*, and *Nick Caine Adventures* (with J.R. Rain). The author has published over thirty books and resides in a small historic town in Tennessee with his wife, Fiona, where they share an old antebellum home with several ghosts.

Please visit his website at: www.aidenjamesfiction.com. Or look for him on Facebook (Aiden James, Paranormal Adventure Author) and on Twitter (@AidenJames3).

Printed in Great Britain
by Amazon.co.uk, Ltd.,
Marston Gate.